PRAISE FOR

The Story of a Million Years

"One of Huddle's finest achievements is to have convinced us of his
characters' complexities without ever needing to declare them interesting, and to have delineated their various voices without re-
sorting to crudely obvious variations in speaking style or personal
obsession . . . Indeed, *The Story of a Million Years* doesn't flaunt its
luster, except insofar as its depth is as faceted as its surface, and it's
not a performance; it doesn't fall back on hat tricks and acrobatics
and doesn't court applause. But that doesn't mean it doesn't deserve
a standing ovation." — *Newsday*

"A stunning first novel . . . Mr. Huddle's characters are marvelously
drawn . . . this book is a wonder. It was impossible to put down
during an initial reading and even more beguiling the second time
around." — *Wall Street Journal*

"Beautiful, accomplished . . . Huddle has imagined and reimagined
his story with understated precision . . . The longer you spend in the
company of each of these narrators, the more deeply identified you
become with each of their dissonant perspectives. This prismatic
richness is cumulative. Over and over again, the voices of *The Story
of a Million Years* inform us of the chiaroscuro of the modern world
— a place of light and shadow and endless possibility, where things
are never merely as they seem." — *Boston Globe*

"An exacting portrait of two couples and their shared histories, de-
sires, and secrets." — *The New Yorker*

"An absorbing book . . . *The Story of a Million Years* is a study in the
way secrets cobweb within relationships, engendering a sharp-edged
loneliness between people who think they know each other . . . This

beautiful and moving book celebrates — and inspires — the desire for understanding in all of us. Call it what you will — *The Story of a Million Years* is a great piece of literature." — ***Orlando Sentinel***

"A shimmering debut novel . . . like a shattered mirror pieced painstakingly together, every shard captures a different angle . . . His view of the human condition brims with wisdom, compassion, and a rare grace." — ***Publishers Weekly***

"Impressively subtle . . . indeed, Huddle's plain language could hardly be further from Nabokov's breathtaking, lepidopterous flight of words. However, the two books share a yearning for the ideals of love and an elegiac vision of the passage of time."
— ***New York Times Book Review***

"A masterful tapestry of characters and narratives."
— ***Richmond Times-Dispatch***

"With each turn from voice to voice, the novel deepens, the web gets stronger, our understanding of the characters gets richer, and our judgments weaken. Still, it is clear in the end what leads to happiness and what leads to the soul's perdition." — ***Los Angeles Times***

The Story
of a
Million Years

Books by David Huddle

A Dream with No Stump Roots in It

Paper Boy

Only the Little Bone

Stopping by Home

The High Spirits: Stories of Men
and Women

The Writing Habit: Essays

The Nature of Yearning

Intimates

A David Huddle Reader

Tenorman: A Novella

Summer Lake: New and Selected Poems

The Story of a Million Years

The Story
of a
Million Years

David Huddle

A Mariner Book
HOUGHTON MIFFLIN COMPANY
BOSTON · NEW YORK

First Mariner Books edition 2000

Copyright © 1999 by David Huddle
ALL RIGHTS RESERVED

For information about permission to reproduce selections from
this book, write to Permissions, Houghton Mifflin Company,
215 Park Avenue South, New York, New York 10003.

Visit our Web site: www.houghtonmifflinbooks.com

Library of Congress Cataloging-in-Publication Data
Huddle, David, date.
The story of a million years / David Huddle.
p.   cm.
ISBN 0-395-96605-1
ISBN 0-618-08233-6 (pbk.)
I. Title.
PS3558.U287S74   1999
813'.54 — dc21   99-32213 CIP

Printed in the United States of America

Book design by Robert Overholtzer

QUM 10 9 8 7 6 5 4 3 2 1

Portions of this novel have appeared in *Five Points, Glimmer
Train, Story,* and *The Best American Short Stories 1996.*

For Bill Clegg

Thanks to Ghita Orth for invaluable criticism and unwavering encouragement; to Lois Rosenthal for faith and a timely recommendation; Cory Wickwire Halaby for the right words at the right time; Janet Silver and Heidi Pitlor for astonishing editorial attention; Frances Apt for sublime manuscript editing; Natalie Norman for more than one good story; and Lindsey, Bess, and Molly Huddle for loving patience, practical help, and inspiring company.

Contents

The Story
of a
Million Years

1

Past My Future

A FEW WEEKS AFTER my fifteenth birthday, a friend of my parents, a Mr. Gordon, asked me — quietly and directly — if I would like to have an adventure with him. He asked his question on a sunny afternoon while he and I sat together at the edge of my family's swimming pool, splashing our feet and talking. Mrs. Gordon sat with my mother a few yards away; they were tanning themselves and chatting. I appreciated how quietly Mr. Gordon spoke. Only I could hear him. Of course I knew that if I wished, I could brush his question aside as more of his teasing. But I knew, too, that if I let my mother and Mrs. Gordon know what he had just said, he would be in trouble.

I told him yes — a yes just as quiet and direct as his question. There came a pause in our conversation — and in our kicking of the swimming pool water — during which he and I kept looking at each other. I noticed Mr. Gordon had shaved closely and recently. It pleased me to think maybe he'd done that for me.

He said, "Well." And I said, "Well?" And he said, "Well, Marcy, I shall be in touch with you."

Thinking about that day and those few minutes of conversation beside the pool, I ask myself if I understood exactly what he had in mind. I wasn't an infant. And I was very well aware that he was married to my mother's friend. But to be perfectly frank, I wanted my adventure with Mr. Gordon to be a sexual one.

Not long before, I'd read some magazine articles that my parents had given me and parts of the books that they'd hidden away from me. One night, months earlier, I was supposed to be attending a country club dance; instead, I was walking around the golf course and smoking cigarettes with a boy. He and I had some very exciting kissing, which led, logically, to his putting his hand on my breast.

If he hadn't gotten nervous and laughed about what we were doing — which I took to mean that he was laughing at my breast — that boy could have gone a lot further with me than he did. Had he whispered that he wanted me to take off my clothes, I would have taken them off. I'd had no experience with that kind of intensity; it took only a few moments for me to reach the point of being vulnerable to the boy. When you're older, you learn to stop short of that point or else to move to it as quickly as possible; that night I was intoxicated by what I hadn't ever felt before. The boy was a year ahead of me in school, but the next day, when I thought about what we'd done, I understood that he had no more experience than I and probably even less knowledge.

I would have tried whatever he knew enough about to ask for. Instead of a request, I got his inane whinny of a laugh.

I was still trying to get used to my breasts. One seemed to be ahead of the other, which, for all I knew, made them comical. But I felt certain that even if they were, Mr. Gordon wouldn't laugh. He had always paid reserved attention to me, had brought me presents, had once even called me from Singapore to wish me happy birthday. Whereas someone my own age would casually humiliate me, Mr. Gordon had for years been offering me careful respect. So I said yes.

When you go into a room with one other person and lock the door behind you, you are momentarily free of every principle by which people ordinarily speak and act with each other. How you're going to be — what you say and do, what you think and feel — with that person is entirely up to the two of you. You may legislate as you wish. I learned that from spending a number of afternoons in a seventh-floor view-of-the-lake sublet in Marsden Towers. Because I was on the track team at school, my parents didn't question me about how I spent my afternoons. I actually had quite a bit of time available to spend with Robert in the apartment he'd rented for us. In those rooms I felt free and strong, which was why I kept wanting to go back there for as long as I did.

The world would have me feel that what Robert and I did was wrong. As if he'd committed a crime against me beyond even what is considered acceptably criminal. I refuse to feel that wrongness. Robert harmed me no more than I harmed him.

I realize now that my mother worked at being friends with Suzanne Gordon. I realize now my mother had a very restrained crush on Robert — a little like the one she had on Jack Kennedy. Robert was accustomed to being flattered by others. To my mother, he made himself entertaining, as he probably did to anyone who courted him. My mother and Robert had grown up together in Shaker Heights; in the past, whenever they were together, they had enjoyed discussing the lives of their childhood acquaintances. Robert and my father had a formal relationship that was played out in terms that amused my mother and me. We teased my bookish father about the stilted conversations he and Robert carried on when they were required to chat. Mostly they discussed tennis, which Robert played regularly but didn't keep up with, and which my father didn't play but kept up with. My father had no real interest in tennis; it was just that every day of his life he read the *Plain Dealer* very thoroughly.

There was a subtlety to the way my mother and Suzanne Gordon related to each other, a warmth that was half real and half pretended. To me, their conversations always sounded nervous. Having thought about her all these years, I've decided that Suzanne was never able to locate herself properly in life, though she was an astute and able person. When I was growing up, I remembered things Suzanne said, and I thought about her a lot. She had no job; she had no children. Though she volunteered at the hospital and the library, she made no friends among the other volunteers. Her manner was too distant, and her conversation was probably too peculiar. My mother said she thought Suzanne spent hours of her life paging through books from museums. I've come to understand that what fascinated me about Suzanne was how alone she seemed — and how it didn't, apparently, bother her that she had no real friends.

The interest she had in Robert, however, she was able to share with my mother. Each knew where the other stood, though I believe that neither ever spoke frankly. As a young child, I'd studied the way my mother and Suzanne talked. They sat with their backs straight in their chairs, their ankles crossed and their hands in their laps, their faces pleasant. Such a formal pose perfectly suited Suzanne; I still have vivid memories of her sitting like that in our living room, with the light from our bay window catching the reddish highlights of her hair. I could sense the awkwardness of her talk with my mother when they took up certain topics they felt obliged to discuss — such as my father, whom my mother wasn't comfortable discussing and in whom Suzanne had no interest. But when they managed to bring the conversation around to the subject of their mutual passion, they became animated, witty, and amused, even slouchy and unladylike in their postures.

"Robert actually laughed at that joke?" my mother might ask, sitting forward in her chair.

Suzanne's laughter would lilt through our house. "Not only did he laugh at it. Last night he told the same joke to Nick Shelton in this disgusting . . ."

I took these exchanges as the proper way for grown-up women to converse. They put on little shows for each other. I didn't want to be like that, but I thought it probably happened as you got older — you gradually became more artificial. It made me cringe to think that out in my future I had similar conversations awaiting me.

As I imagine most men do, Robert struggled to balance his appetite with his stamina. He was, however, a master of sustaining the illusion of vast possibility within the circumstances of sexual intimacy. He and I did nothing especially strange or hurtful or even, for that matter, adventuresome. I was fifteen. He was forty-one. For a while, that alone was adventure enough for each of us. At first, Robert liked to say that if it weren't for those twenty-six years between us, we'd have no interest in each other. He seemed to be practicing a joke he might tell people if he and I ever went out together in public: "You know, if Marcy and I didn't have that twenty-six-year difference . . ." I was glad when he stopped saying it to me.

We did not go out together. Ever.

The project we undertook was informing each other about ourselves. He didn't say so, but I think Robert hoped I would teach him how it was to live in my mind and my body. He anticipated the questions I wished him to ask me. He knew when to be quiet and let me talk. Or when to let me think through what I had just told him aloud until I came to the next thing I wanted to tell him. He knew when to interrupt me, to get me excited, to make me try to answer four questions at once. Whatever he wanted to know about me, I was eager to tell.

Once he asked, "So do you think you'll want to have children?"

I didn't have to think for even an instant. "Of course I will!" I blurted. The moment I spoke those words, I knew them to be true. But it struck me as odd that Robert had to force himself to smile and that he didn't ask how many I wanted or whether I'd prefer boys or girls.

"Let the commerce commence," Robert liked to say in his booming voice upon entering our little foyer at Marsden Towers. I understood him to mean both our talk and our sex. Mostly, Robert asked questions and I answered them. During these conversations, we undressed, we kissed, we nuzzled, we stroked; after a while I understood that we were talking as a way to extend the sex, to stretch it out, make it last. Like Robert's fingers, our words and sentences brushed over my skin. Or maybe *instead* of Robert's fingers. When I let myself actually watch his fingers moving across my breasts or up along my thighs, I didn't like it nearly as much as keeping my eyes shut while we talked and his hands did what they did. I liked that part more than I ever told him. So the talk, for me, became the best part of the sex. The commerce could also change into the silences we let pass when we were simply breathing with each other in the afternoon sunlight that shone on our bed. We concentrated on not talking, because the silence had become what would make the sex last. There were times when that, too, was exactly what I wanted.

Though his curiosity about me was his first interest, Robert also wanted me to know how it felt to be him, to live in his mind, his body. These topics weren't anything I had a natural curiosity about; what I most wanted him to talk about was his wife, but he was reluctant to do so. If I asked a question about Suzanne, he would answer so carefully that I could almost feel him searching for the most neutral phrasing. Sometimes he'd finish up his answer with "Why do you want to know?" I hated that. I always told him, "Oh, just because . . ." I'm not sure I knew it at the time, but I know now that I wanted Robert to describe making love to Suzanne — what little things she might say, what she liked, even how she might sigh or whimper. I wanted to compare myself with Suzanne. But that, of course, was exactly the kind of information Robert wasn't about to give me. And I didn't want him to know I had such a squalid curiosity.

So I asked questions about "the adult world" — as if it were a scientific topic. I did have a vague curiosity about being grown up, or perhaps I had a need to vent my complaints about grown-ups. Robert listened to me; sometimes he agreed; sometimes he sided with the teacher or the parent I was criticizing. He asked me not to categorize him as "an adult."

One afternoon he told me, "Think of the bodies of human beings as cars. We can't see each other's interiors. Cars see other cars. I'm a station wagon. You're a sports car, but you have your top up so that I can't see who's driving. All I see is this little red MG streaking past me on the turnpike. I think to myself, My goodness, I wish I could be like that MG. But the thing about it is, I'm exactly like that MG. Except that I got put behind the wheel of this station wagon — this middle-aged body with a middle-aged male mind under the hood — and I can't get out. I have to keep driving the equipment I've been given. But who's driving each one of us is this androgynous blob of a creature, one per car, each the same as the others. The driver of my car is exactly like the driver of your car.

"These creatures don't age. They're neutral creatures, and they're impatient with their cars for having such limited equipment. Mine thinks I'm silly to worry so much about you getting home on time. But it understands that I'm given to worrying. And yours probably wishes you'd keep your eye on the clock so as not to risk having your parents quiz you about where you've been. It knows precisely how flimsy that excuse of yours is — 'Coach made me stay late.' If my inner being could talk to your inner being, the two would immediately recognize that they're identical. Right away they'd start criticizing us to each other. Mine would say, 'I'll swear, Robert is so damn middle-aged sometimes. He just about drives me nuts.' And yours would say, 'I know exactly what you mean. The other day Marcy went shopping with her mother, and you wouldn't believe how she spoke to . . .'"

We were always engaged in whatever we were talking about. I've come to know he was quite an imaginative man, though when I was with him, he did not seem remarkable in that way. It was that he so much liked talking with me that he made our conversations interesting. He found ways to do that. And the ways he found came about from his figuring out what would entertain me or interest me or pique my curiosity. He didn't ever condescend; I had a sense of conversing with him, as if the two of us were talking our way toward some destination.

Here is something Robert told me he thought a young woman should know: if you think a man might be interested in you but you're not sure, find an occasion to sit close to him. Go with this man to a lecture, say, or a reading, something in an auditorium, preferably not a movie or a play, both of which can be distracting. Unobtrusively fix yourself not to be touching him but to be very nearly so. If possible, align your upper arm with his upper arm, not touching, of course, but approximately an inch apart. It's simple. If he has no interest in you, there will be nothing to notice. If he's interested, you will feel a certain warmth coming from his body. If he's extremely interested, you'll be surprised that his body would so overtly and crudely give him away.

In a man's mind, even when it's clear that he wants a woman to be thinking about him, he would prefer her not to know the extent of his liking her. His body, however, will always reveal how much or how little interest he has. Arranging the appropriate seating is the only difficulty. The man who knows this secret may, even as you're trying to find out about him, easily measure your own interest. Robert even claimed to be certain his own body had given him away once when I was fourteen and he and I were alone in my parents' living room. But of course I couldn't have known that at the time.

And whether or not his little lesson was a useful one, I couldn't say. I've never had an occasion when I thought to test it.

We ended because of a boy. I shouldn't be ashamed of that, though I think of this as the way I betrayed Robert. A boy my own age. I began talking to Robert about this boy. For a while I wasn't aware of what I might be revealing. I was simply telling him about school, and Allen Crandall kept coming up in my conversation. I heard myself say his name, again and again. And I watched Robert as I said it.

My saying it so often must have made me realize I liked Allen Crandall. He was an athlete who moved through the hallways with a swagger. Allen wasn't afraid to disagree even with those teachers who got mad if you disagreed with them. Sometimes I saw Allen looking at me as if he knew something amusing about me, though I knew he didn't. As I talked more and more about him to Robert, I began to notice a hardening of Robert's face, so I tried to hush myself up. By that time — or well before — Robert had sensed my interest in Allen and began to question me.

A sadness came into Robert's voice — even into his body — that I hated.

The sadness actually became Robert's oldness. For more than a year, I hadn't paid much attention to his age, but now it seemed evident in everything about him. His face, his clothes, the way he talked and combed his hair and rubbed his temples when he was tired. Even the way he smelled. He had an expensive cologne-deodorant-soap fragrance about him that I'd loved from back in my childhood, but now it began to bother me. When he bought me presents, usually clothes that no one my age would ever wear, they embarrassed me. Everything about Robert seemed inescapably sad. He made me think of my father, alone in the house on Sunday afternoons and listening to one of his classical records turned up loud the way he liked.

The commerce had become almost completely conversation — and conversation that neither Robert nor I seemed to enjoy. Quickly after I started talking so much about Allen, the commerce had changed.

"Let the commerce commence!" I called out one afternoon when I burst into the room, exhilarated from my day at school. As I came in, Robert was walking toward me in the little foyer. I knew he had in mind to give me one of his sad hugs, where it felt as if he was trying to wrap me up with him in his suit jacket. That day I was standing close enough to him to notice his wince the instant I'd made my joke.

To his credit, Robert managed to stay just far enough ahead of me to know how I felt. One rainy afternoon I walked to Marsden Towers, thinking I had to make myself tell him I wasn't going to be coming back anymore. Just as I set my hand to knock, he swung open the door. He was cheerful, teasing, impeccably dressed in a new suit and shirt and brightly striped tie. Usually he took his suit jacket off while he waited for me to arrive, but not today. He wore it buttoned, and for a moment or two he was as dazzling to me as when I'd been a young girl looking up at this grand visitor to our house. When he kissed me on both cheeks and then my forehead, I noticed that his shoes had been freshly polished.

"I'm setting you free, my dear," he said. "Our adventure has reached its conclusion." He had fancy glasses on a tray and champagne for himself and Perrier with a dish of lemon slices for me. He poured the glasses full, handed me mine, and lifted his to me. "This has been lovely, Marcy," he said. "I can't begin to tell you."

He planned to say more, and I wanted to help him say it. I lifted my glass to him, too, and our glasses made the little tink that seems so celebratory when you're in a happy mood. Though he opened his mouth to go on, he couldn't. Just before he turned to the window, he began swatting the air in front of his face. I thought he might be about to sneeze or that he was trying to wave away some insect buzzing at him. Then, with his back to me, he made a noise. Or I saw his shoulders move, and I imagined that he made a noise.

I knew.

"All right, Robert." I set my glass back down on the tray. "Thank you," I said. When I tried to think of more to say, I found nothing but what the kids say to each other in the halls at school — *See you later. I'll call you tonight. Take it easy.* So I kept quiet and touched the back of his suit jacket. I brushed my hand down his back just a bit. Just enough to feel how much he didn't want me to touch him.

And I knew, then, to leave the room.

As a child, I was sometimes awakened by my parents making love. My room was across the hall from theirs, and often what woke me was one of them getting up to close their door. I could hear only faint noises, their voices more like humming than talking. But even with the door muffling their words, I could distinguish something different in their tones, a new sound, a quality that I didn't hear in their ordinary conversation — like a sound each made especially for the other, as if softly singing.

Sometimes either they forgot about the door being open or they thought it was too deep into the night for me to be awake. At any rate, they'd leave it open, and I could listen carefully. I was greedy to hear them. I don't know how old I was when I realized what they must be doing. When I was very little, of course, I must have had no idea what they were up to. But I don't remember that. I remember only knowing what the noise meant and wanting to hear every single bit of it.

I've read about children being drawn to the sounds of their parents' love-making, but I wasn't ever tempted to interrupt them. I stayed very quiet, because I wanted them to reach their conclusion. That was marked by my father's restrained shout — into the pillow, I suppose — "Oh, oh! Oh, my darling," he'd say.

I loved that. I loved his calling out. My father is long dead now, but remembering his voice like that still makes me smile.

As an adult, I've thought about what I heard. I've wondered, for instance, about the extent of my mother's satisfaction. None of the noises I ever heard suggested she reached orgasm during their intercourse, though the sounds she made did suggest that her intercourse with my father was something she liked. And she always seemed to me to be aware of her sexuality. So what did she do? Masturbate when no one was around? Go without orgasms altogether? In those days there wasn't much sex, I'm tempted to say, but of course that would be wrong. Enlightened sex is what there wasn't much of. And I could be wrong about that, too. Publicly, she was a bit of a prude; it's possible she faked not having orgasms. I suppose it's rude to wonder very much about your mother's coming.

Also, I wonder what effect eavesdropping on their love-making had on me. Did it make me overly interested in sex? Had my parents awakened me and insisted that I listen, that would have been sexual abuse. But of course it was very nearly the same experience, my listening to them so carefully from across the hallway. Did it, for instance, make me vulnerable to Robert when he posed his question to me by the pool? Would I have so readily known what Robert meant if I hadn't had this education, so to speak? Would I have said yes so readily?

Not so long ago, when my friend Uta and I were talking, we came to the topic of our parents' sex lives. I told her I'd often overheard my parents doing it. When I asked Uta what effect she thought that may have had on me, she said, "I don't know, Marcy. I can tell you that never in all my life did I see or hear any evidence that my parents even had sex lives. If you ask me, that was much worse than what you're talking about. I sometimes wonder how I ever got my feet on this planet. At least you know how you got here. At least you know your parents cared about each other enough to do it."

I told Uta she had a point.

A few afternoons when he thought I would be home by myself, Robert called and attempted to chat, politely, about how things were going for me. This was after our last meeting at Marsden Towers, and though I didn't wish them to be, these calls were awkward occasions. Neither of us was able to relax into conversation.

On an afternoon when Allen Crandall had come home with me, ostensibly to study for an exam, Robert called.

It was spring, near the end of May. Allen and I were full of ourselves and more than a little silly, with the end of the school year approaching and with our discovery of each other. I was just finding out how it was to be with somebody that way, with our moods and our voices so perfectly matched. We were gossiping about our classmates and mocking them and laughing a great deal while we walked around my house, drinking soda and munching on chips and crackers from the kitchen. I was catching on, then, to the way Allen talked, a clipped, half-joking way of saying everything. When the phone rang, I had no doubt who the caller was. The instant I heard myself say hello — with the fun still in my voice but also a bit of the dread I felt at having to carry on even a short conversation with him — I knew Robert would know that Allen was with me.

There was the slightest pause. Then Robert's voice came through the receiver: "Hello, Marcy. I hope you're well. I'll call you back another time."

I said, "All right." The line went dead.

And of course Allen asked who it was. Instantly, I had to

make up something to tell him. "My mom," I said. "She wants me to . . . set out some eggs." I went to the refrigerator, removed a tray of brown eggs, and set them on the counter.

When I turned to him, Allen was looking at me with his head tilted. He gave it a little shake and said, "Speaking of eggs, you think we ought to crack those books?"

I said, "Nah." And I went toward him, meaning to tickle him. I wanted to recover the mood we'd been in before the phone rang.

"Weird over here at your house," Allen said, dodging my attack. "Your mom calls and you get sad. You say 'All right,' hang up the phone, then go to the refrigerator and set out a tray of eggs. Weird."

I stopped trying to tickle him. "You haven't seen anything yet, my dear," I said. "My dear" coming out of my mouth made my face turn hot; it was Robert's phrase, not mine. But I was determined not to let Robert's phone call ruin my afternoon with Allen. I began picking up things throughout the house and setting them in odd places. I carried a magazine from the living room to the kitchen, where I put it in the refrigerator; I plucked down my father's ski hat from the closet and arranged it as the centerpiece of the dining room table; I asked Allen to take off his loafers, which I then ceremoniously carried back to the kitchen and placed in the sink. Allen was kind enough to over-look my desperation in trying to amuse him. He let himself be amused, and soon we'd recovered the spirit of kidding around.

That day I decided I wouldn't ever, under any circumstances, tell Allen about Robert and me. Why that day? I suppose be-cause I saw myself taking a great deal of trouble to disguise the fact that my former lover had called me. I realized that even having a former lover, no less a man almost three times as old as I was, wasn't something I wanted anybody my age to know.

You'd think — since I married him — a time would have come when I could tell Allen all about Robert.

Such a time did not ever arrive.

The swimming pool, the commerce — the way we ordered take-out food brought to us and ate it while the commerce went on — how Robert and I were with each other was this intricate and intense part of my life. I wouldn't give it to Allen. I wanted to hold it entirely to myself — whether from embarrassment or selfishness, I have never been able to decide.

For many months I kept expecting to see Robert. I knew he was having to maneuver to keep from encountering me when he socialized with my parents. He did manage that. If he and Suzanne came to our house, it was at a time when I wouldn't be there. And somehow he kept those occasions to a minimum. When my parents saw the Gordons, it was at a party at someone else's house, at a restaurant, or at the Gordons' house. My mother was aware that Robert and Suzanne weren't at our house nearly as often as in previous years, but it wasn't something she chose to discuss with me. I knew she was keeping it to herself, and I might have been a little irked about that. I do recall a conversation between my parents; my mother said, "We don't seem as close to them as we used to be," and my father said, "Oh? I hadn't noticed any change." Since they'd been talking about something else at the time, they let the topic of the Gordons drop, which suited me well enough, because my pulse had picked up in a way that made me uncomfortable.

I've always had trouble giving it a name — affair, relationship, arrangement, liaison. I still don't know what to call it. At any rate, in the first months after Robert and I ended whatever it was, I dreaded seeing him. And I thought he might try to see me. When it became apparent that he didn't want to see me, I began wanting to see him. I wasn't sure why.

I certainly didn't want to talk with Robert; the telephone conversations we'd attempted made me feel as if I'd done something awful to him. So even though talking had been what I most valued about being with him, I knew I wasn't after any more talk. But now I did want to see him, and not just his face, but the whole of him. As if my eyes had to take hold of him.

Maybe, more truthfully, what I wanted was for him to look at me and for me to see what his face would tell me about who I had become.

For a while I entertained a fantasy that Robert came into our house one of the afternoons when I was alone. He simply walked in. From the living room, where I sat, I saw him and wasn't surprised or frightened. He was dressed as he was when I'd seen him last, in one of his dark business suits, with a white shirt and a bright tie. With his hands in his jacket pockets, he stood in our foyer, looking at me, neither frowning nor smiling. I returned his stare. Then he took his hands from his pockets and made that downward movement, fluttering his fingers, as if he were miming the way leaves would fall from a tree. In our rooms at Marsden Towers, that gesture meant that he wished me to take off my clothes.

By that time — I was sixteen — I knew more about my body and had come to think that how it looked didn't have much to do with who I actually was. I was thin, and my legs were perfectly muscled, but how they could *move* was what really mattered. For my school's track team I did the 100- and 220-yard dashes. My body's strength and quickness were what I loved. I became irritated when people made so much of how it looked. So in this fantasy, I said, "No, Robert. That isn't possible." My voice had a sternness I had never used with him. I remained sitting. Robert said nothing. He merely nodded, looked wistful, turned, and left the house.

When I knew he was gone, I tiptoed quickly to the door, locked it, and stood with my back braced against it.

This moment of my back against the door felt like something that was really going to come to me, a little treasure. For months, I found myself moving through this daydream, refining it, taking a peculiar comfort from it.

One evening my parents invited Allen Crandall to join us for dinner at Forlini's, a noisy place that had taken over the bottom floor of one of the city's old department stores. The dining area was so enormous that on a busy night it was like a circus tent. Waiters and waitresses ran, busboys and busgirls ran, even the two hostesses ran and smiled and shouted among the tables of people as if they were running an obstacle course for clowns. My parents liked Forlini's because the crowd was young and stylish; my father said it gave us a preview of the people who would be running the city in another ten years. My mother and I enjoyed the spectacle, seeing so many people all at once, not to mention the zipping back and forth of the waiters and waitresses, who all wore khaki shorts and red T-shirts and must have been hired for their lively appearance. Allen had never been to Forlini's before; ordinarily, he would have concentrated on practicing his conversational skills with my parents, but this evening he was nearly overwhelmed by the thick hum of voices, all those bodies, and their laughing, talking, feeding faces. The four of us sat at our table, gawking at the people around us.

"Is that Robert? Isn't that Robert and Suzanne?" my mother asked my father. She was sitting up straight in her chair and squinting across the room.

A splash of ice water down my back might have been less

shocking. And some part of me was oddly angry that my mother had addressed her question only to my father. To her, my acquaintance with Robert meant so little, she didn't think to ask me. That angry part of myself seemed a distinct and dangerous person at the moment. She was a Marcy who wanted to smack the restaurant table hard enough to make the flatware clatter. She was a Marcy who wanted to make a speech to her parents, to Allen, even to the diners near us: "Is that Robert Gordon? Well, Mother, why don't you ask me? I'm the one whose fingertips have touched every square inch of that man's body. I expect I am the one you should ask whether the man you're looking at is Robert."

What that Marcy wanted to prove with such a speech was beyond my knowing. As quickly as she'd come close to bursting into the open, she withdrew to my prudent self. I was, in fact, being so prudent that I couldn't make myself turn directly toward where my mother was straining to see. Then she must have remembered I could recognize Robert, too, because she said, "Right there, Marcy." Since she was sitting beside me, and I wasn't looking the right way, my mother actually pulled my chin to turn my head in the proper direction.

So I saw him.

My mother continued to hold my head turned toward Robert as if she thought she had to help me see him. My sight seemed to soar across the room and cast light on him. So clearly did I see his face that I noticed a ripple of tension pass from his temple down along his jawline. I saw him squint to make out what peculiar thing my mother was doing to my head. I saw him half lift one hand toward us, as if to wave or signal my mother to loosen her hold on me. His other hand stayed on Suzanne's upper arm as they moved toward the steps that led up and out of the restaurant.

What disturbed me was how Robert's body and Suzanne's body were so well matched. Robert had dressed down for the evening, in a dark golf shirt and chinos. His thin chest and thick waist were much more visible than when he wore a suit. Suzanne's dress somehow accentuated how age had softened her figure. Anyone else looking at the couple leaving the restaurant probably wouldn't have noticed their bodies at all, but I couldn't help it. The two of them were connected by how their bodies were placed in time; I saw that as clearly as when I suddenly realize I've been watching the male and female in a pair of birds. In Robert and Suzanne, this was not something I wanted to see. My stomach went into a spasm, as if I were watching them undress.

Red-capped and bandana-ed cooks shoved pizzas and casserole dishes into wood-burning ovens while they shouted to each other and to the waiters and waitresses. Robert and Suzanne were far across the cavernous room, which swelled and echoed with the raucous voices of hundreds of people. A woman at a table near us laughed at a very high pitch; she seemed unable to stop herself. Near Robert and Suzanne a man stood up and waved both arms to get someone's attention. An Edith Piaf song played stridently over the sound system. Even the ceiling lights appeared to flicker.

He was much paler than I'd ever seen him, which made me suspect that during the months of our meetings at Marsden Towers he'd been using a tanning lamp. I wondered why I hadn't noticed it at the time.

Robert continued to move away from me even as he kept his face turned toward me. It looked as if he was almost pushing Suzanne to the exit. Though he knew me well enough to know I would never make a scene, he must have been terrified that I'd approach him in front of his wife; terrified that I might say hello to him.

A fury lit up inside me — and died almost immediately. Had I been close enough in that single instant, I would have spat on him.

I've tried to forgive Robert his cowardice of that evening. I don't think I've managed it. I saw, in his pale face, eyes staring at me across the room, that with his wife beside him he couldn't stand to speak to me.

So he ran from a child.

Of course he had to turn his face away from me. When Robert did that — when he gave me the back of his thin shoulders to see — I felt released. I felt as if I had just beaten him at something, and suddenly became aware that I'd half risen from my chair and that my parents and my boyfriend were staring at me. Easing back into my seat, I turned and found three frozen faces. Allen had even paused in chewing his food. I knew our lives depended on what I did next. It took all my strength to smile at Allen and resume eating.

2

Past Perfect

MARCY will look you straight in the face and tell you that moments come along when you can see what's ahead of you. Openings in time are available, she will tell you, and if you're alert, you can catch glimpses of the future. That's how she is these days — a little spooky.

Believe me, though, I know how Marcy can be. When she and I were in high school, she had an intensity that scared everybody, especially people her own age. She had unusual powers of concentration. Marcy Bunkleman lived in the moment more than any person I've ever known. She didn't try to do it, and she didn't have a philosophy about it; she just naturally lived that way — all-out alert and awake in whatever she was doing. Which quality made her, among other things, a remarkable athlete. That girl could run like a cheetah. Seeing her run in practice a few times made me understand what the girl had. That concentration — it was the same thing I had in baseball, except that I had to work at it, will it into place; whereas Marcy had it with her all the time, standard equipment. Kids that age have trouble focusing, but it was easy for Marcy; it was what she liked to do. And of course she made good grades — she never even understood what it meant to have trouble with your schoolwork. Her teachers thought her a notch or two short of being a genius; they were horrified when Marcy let it be known that after graduation she wanted to go to nursing school.

Spring sport season was when I met her; she was on the track team, and I played baseball. We got out of practice just about the time the girls' track team came down to the field. I talked their coach into giving me a stopwatch and letting me time the girls' practice heats. That way it was easy to strike up a conversation with Marcy. March is a crazy time for outdoor sports, especially in Cleveland, with all the weather that comes in off the lake. A single afternoon can turn from sunny and warm to blowing snow. Girls in track shorts in chilly weather were just about the sexiest sight I could think of in those days.

One afternoon, the two of us were out there, jumping up and down to try to keep warm in the cold wind. "Got a jacket here I don't mind lending you," I said.

"That's your letter jacket. That's a baseball jacket," she said, giving me a disdainful look that I took seriously for a moment. "I can't wear that. A big jacket like that would slow me down. Coach would throw me off the team."

I rolled my eyes at her, and she gave me back this impish look. "Baseball guys can't run," she said. "Don't you know that?" She went on with her hopping up and down.

"Tell you what," I said. "You put this jacket on. I guarantee you, not only will you be warmer, but you'll also increase your speed by a minimum of thirty percent."

She stopped hopping just like that and stepped straight up to me. "Hand it over," she said. "If you're wrong about the increased speed, I'm going to take the thing off and walk on it. I'm going to stomp it into the mud."

The way she said it, I wasn't certain she was kidding, but I handed her the jacket. "Yes, ma'am," I said. Her eyes were on me like she could see all the way through to my bones — and I saw she was grinning at me. She was right there — very intense — and of course I couldn't help grinning back at her. Later on, I realized what it was about her. She was so alert that there wasn't a boy in our school who had the nerve to talk to her face to face. And I'm not talking about her looks; I'm talking about her general state of consciousness. People were drawn to her, but they had to keep their distance.

Not me. What I had — the little gift that came down to me from the old Crandall clan of Scotland — was another thing altogether. In high school I was a very bright guy. In retrospect, I understand that I wasn't nearly the genius I fancied myself to be, but I had the ability to grasp the big picture. This was of particular value in baseball — especially applicable to the science of hitting a baseball. My basic athletic skills — quickness, speed, coordination, all those things — were a little above average, but what I could do better than anybody my age was anticipate what a pitcher was going to throw and where he was going to throw it. Funniest thing: my hitting ability was directly proportional to the skills of the pitcher I was facing. The better the pitcher, the better I could hit him. He had to know what he was doing before I could know what he was doing.

I lacked modesty in those days. And I won't claim to have acquired an excess amount of it as an adult. In my opinion, it isn't fair to expect people with resources to act as if they don't know what they have. But I'm not an athlete anymore, and I have gained some perspective. I can look back on those old high school days and see pretty clearly that Marcy and I were bound to come together. I was a year ahead of her, but the two of us were, in a way, isolated from our classmates. To me it felt like the two of us were grown-ups disguised to look like the kids who surrounded us. I used to say — even though she didn't like to hear it — that she and I were the only two human beings walking around in a huge herd of aliens. If I hadn't struck up that conversation with her during track practice, we'd probably have found another way to meet. I mean, just passing in the hallway, we might have caught each other's eyes and recognized that we were more like each other than we were like anybody else in that school.

When we first got to know each other, I wasn't *romantically* interested in Marcy; I was just excited to have somebody to talk to. There wasn't anybody else. I didn't have brothers and sisters; I didn't get along with the kids in my neighborhood; my class-mates were either dummies who hated me or dummies who were envious of me; my teachers respected me, but thought I was too big for my britches — I was, but that didn't mean I couldn't have used a little friendly interest from them — and my parents were so totally caught up in being the parents of a prodigy that talking to them was out of the question. At the time, I wasn't aware of it — and I was probably too immodest to admit it even to myself — but I was a lonely boy.

So along comes Marcy Bunkleman, chilly in the March wind and needing to borrow somebody's letter jacket to keep warm. It wasn't only that she and I had things to talk about, things in common, things we'd never said out loud to anybody. It was also timing. She and I had a *rhythmic* understanding of each other. She'd say this ("Your jacket's got a little fragrance to it, don't you think?") — I'd say that ("That's the smell of pure speed. That's the smell of victory"). She'd talk along a while ("Oh yes, speed, I know all about that . . .") — I'd grunt ("Uh huh —"). She'd talk a little more, and then it was my turn, and she'd listen, nod, shake her head. Like that. We sometimes even hit the silences just right. Some warped little piece of time would come along when neither of us would say a word; we'd each give this snorty little laugh to acknowledge that it had happened, and we'd be off again — talk, talk, talk. I mean, who wouldn't have been excited?

But it was more like friendship than anything else; we'd no more have thought about holding hands in the hallways at school than we'd have gotten drunk before going to class. Or standing by our lockers and making out? That idea wouldn't have occurred to either one of us. Whenever we walked any-where together, we kept at least a body's worth of distance between us. That was a really sweet time in both our lives. We were sixteen and seventeen; finally, we'd each found a pal.

Then one afternoon I was over at her house. It wasn't the first time I'd been there, but it might have been the first time with-out her mom or her dad being around. It was late spring, almost time for school to be out. We were in the kitchen — I remember I was eating potato chips and telling Marcy about the other guys on the baseball team. My junior year I was hitting almost .600, and a pro scout had showed up at a couple of our games to watch me. I sometimes had to remind myself that there might be other topics of conversation than the great baseball season I was having. Marcy had had a pretty good season with the track team, too, but it wasn't ninety percent of her life, the way baseball was for me. Anyway, I was deep into my monologue, talking about Bill Norman's stance and Tony Magistrale's swing and how Howard Clegg, our shortstop, if he thought a fastball was coming, bailed out of the box before the pitcher even released the ball, and about how our coach didn't really know hitting, probably hadn't read as many books on it as I had. By that time, I'd gotten relaxed about being alone in the house with Marcy. Her face showed me that she enjoyed the way I talked, so I was letting loose one sentence after another. I could have gone on with my topic for another twenty minutes, except that the phone rang.

Marcy's hello didn't sound like her. I was leaning against the counter at the sink, and she was sitting on a stool opposite me, where the phone was. She just held the receiver to her ear after she said hello, and the kitchen got quiet as a tomb while whoever was on the other end did the talking. It didn't last long, but I could feel my face turning red as I watched her. She bowed her head and squeezed her arms against her body like she was trying to compress herself. It was as if she'd done some awful, secret thing, and this person — whoever it was — was calling her up to inform her that she'd been found out. Of course I knew Marcy well enough to know there wasn't much terrible that she *could* do — or ever would do. Probably I should have walked out of the kitchen and given her some privacy, but I couldn't help standing there and watching. Color sprang into her face, and she blinked as if it wouldn't take much to make her cry. Which I'd never seen her do.

When she set the receiver down, she just sat there, staring at her hands.

I understood that I'd seen her being hurt. And somebody else's pain is always embarrassing — at least, it is for me. I'd almost rather get hurt myself than see it happen to somebody else. The kitchen was completely silent, and I felt really awkward, just standing there. I decided that Marcy and I had to acknowledge this phone call.

I asked her who it was.

It was like she was sitting on a stage, under a spotlight, trying to remember her lines, and I'd whispered a cue to her. All of a sudden she stood up and began moving around the kitchen. She told me it was her mother on the phone and that her

mother had asked her to set out some eggs. She went to the refrigerator, removed a tray of eggs, and put it on the counter
beside me. Then she stepped back, gave me this plastic smile,
and folded her hands in front of her skirt like the next thing she
intended to do was curtsy.

It didn't really count as lying, what she said, because her little
show with the eggs demonstrated pretty clearly she was making
it up. So she meant me to understand that she wasn't about to
tell me who'd been on the other end of the line. And that was
cool with me, because I really didn't have any curiosity about
who it was. As I say, I wasn't "in love" with Marcy, at that
moment anyway, so I wasn't jealous of her. I just wanted the
afternoon to keep moving along the way it had been going
before the phone call.

I said something — I don't remember what it was, some kidding around — and she started kidding around, too, except in
this extravagant kind of way, walking all through the house and
moving things around. She even asked me to take off my shoes,
which she carried over to the kitchen sink. She set my new
loafers into the sink like they were a roast she wanted to defrost.
I mean, it was a strange thing to do, and it was a performance,
sure it was, a little bit of theater, but I didn't think Marcy was
honestly trying to deceive me. She wanted the same thing I
wanted, to get the afternoon moving again after it had come to
such a grinding halt. This was how she was doing it, and she
was including me. There was a part for me in this little play she
was making up.

I was seventeen years old. I can't have known very much
about what goes on in the hearts of other people. To tell the
truth, I hadn't spent a lot of time around girls, probably because most of my time and energy were spent on athletics. The
summer before, at camp, I'd kissed a girl named Allison Jeffords

out on the soccer field, but we'd been too jumpy with each other to get around to making out. So that afternoon over at Marcy's house I had a lot of innocence behind me. Marcy didn't have a lot of experience, either. I knew that because we went to the same school, and believe me, you know a girl's reputation if you go to school with her.

Marcy took her shoes off, too, and put them on the mantelpiece in the living room. Then she and I walked all around the downstairs of her house, like we were taking a little pretend trip. That was when it occurred to me that Marcy must be going through some difficulty; the thing that hurt her was making her act this way. Maybe she *was* acting a little strange, but she was also being funny. She was — how can I say it? — being companionable. I mean, when I thought about it, I could go back and imagine anyone else hanging up the phone, turning to me, and saying, "Allen, I don't feel very well. Could you excuse me please?" and sending me home. She hadn't done that.

The girl had a spirit about her — that's what I was seeing. And I have to say, I was moved. For just a few seconds, I was pulled right up out of myself. I'd had no experience with such a thing. So I committed this act that I probably wouldn't have thought of in normal circumstances. Still in just my socks, I stepped in front of Marcy and put one hand on each of her shoulders.

She was a little startled, because body contact wasn't part of our repertoire, and she'd been moving around the house with a certain amount of energy and purpose. And here, all of a sudden, was my body blocking her way. I was a skinny guy in those days, but I was still a head taller than she was. Later, when I thought about it, I decided it may have been one of Marcy's first intimate encounters with a male body. So she and I were into something absolutely new for both of us — my body and her body saying hello to each other in her empty and suddenly quiet house.

While we stood there, I realized the moment was precarious. It must have been evident to both of us: *This could go one way or another.* The pose we'd taken was more a pre-embrace than an actual one. I had a definite hold on her shoulders, but my forearms weren't quite touching her upper arms. There was a good foot of space between us. Either one of us could have stepped back.

But neither one did.

Her face instructed me that all I had to do was ask her what was wrong, and she would tell me. She would answer whatever question I asked. I mean, I was used to her face; I'd seen it from every angle, outdoors and indoors. I'd seen her happy, and I'd even seen her mad a couple of times out on the track field, when she'd tripped or run a lousy heat. But right then it was as if I was seeing her face for the first time. How to say what was there? What I hadn't seen until then and what I've never seen since? It was an utter openness — like: *Okay, big guy, here you are in front of me, ask me for something and I'll give it to you, no questions asked.* How many times does one person see that in another? Well, I give myself credit; at least I recognized that I was standing in the middle of an exceptional moment.

I opened my mouth to say *What's wrong, Marcy? What's the matter?* But the words didn't come out. Just in time, I realized they didn't have to. When I say that back in those days I had the ability to grasp the big picture, I think it was that aptitude that saved me — or saved us. Here came a pitch I didn't have to swing at. I was right. Later, I saw pretty clearly that if I'd spoken those words aloud, Marcy and I would have had to sit down and talk about it the rest of the afternoon. Whatever it was, the problem, the difficulty, the hard thing she was dealing with, would have taken over our lives. We'd have had to discuss it that day and the next day and the day after that.

So I bowed down a little bit toward her, and she moved up on tiptoe a little bit toward me, and even though our geography wasn't much changed, that was when she and I really did move into an embrace. It happened. I let my arms touch down along hers, she touched her hands — just the fingers — to either side of my waist, and we tilted our heads in opposite directions to bring our mouths together.

Except we didn't.

We just stood that way. Almost kissing. The two of us barely breathing. Marcy wasn't somebody to wear perfume, and I don't think she had on any kind of scent, but her hair still smelled like shampoo and her skin like soap. I have to say, up close like that, she was really something. Even though I was only lightly touching her, I could sense Marcy's whole body kind of humming. And I had this powerful sense of that spirit of hers, that force I'd seen moving her through the house and jump-starting our afternoon after the phone call had stalled it. So I knew I'd done the correct thing. By putting myself in the right place, I'd earned the privilege of this energy, this kindness. It was as if I'd found a way to step into the presence of some incredibly rare creature, a snow leopard or an albino gazelle.

I can save this. That's what I thought. I remember it so clearly. *I can hold on to this. I can keep it.* To tell the truth, I was pretty proud of having such an insight, of being able to make such a decision, and of taking responsibility for everything that came after it. From that moment on, I was in love with Marcy. There wasn't any other way for me to be, after I'd had that experience. Standing with her like that. Almost kissing. It's kind of funny, I guess. Other couples reach marriage because they go in the opposite direction; they really get into the heat of a physical relationship. Often enough, the guy gets the girl pregnant. Kids in our high school had that happen to them all the time, an ordinary thing. But Marcy and I got to be a couple — and a few years later came to be married people and then had our kids and lived out all those hundreds and hundreds of days that we had together — all because of that one afternoon in her parents' house when we almost kissed. We came exactly close enough.

3

A.B.C.

FROM THE GET-GO, my opinion of A.B.C. was not high. A guy trimming his armpit hair makes a first impression only slightly higher than a guy shaving his legs. A.B.C. was handsome enough — and thirty years later, he still has a shadow of choirboy sweetness to his face — but in those days just about every guy at U.Va. was more or less good-looking.

Allen Ballston Crandall came to U.Va. on a baseball scholarship. Fall semester of 1966, the two of us were assigned to second floor Emmett House. My first memory of him is from the big dormitory bathroom down at the end of the hall. I was shaving, and A.B.C. was trimming his armpit hair with what looked like his mother's sewing scissors. When somebody introduced us, our eyes flicked to each other's face in the mirror we were standing in front of, but neither of us made a move to shake hands. You don't, in that circumstance.

Even in that high-vanity atmosphere, A.B.C. struck me as a narcissist. I wasn't alone in my perception. He was rooming with Bob Waters, who had friends all up and down the hall; if you went into their room, like as not you'd find A.B.C. looking in the mirror, tweezing his nostrils or squeezing a blackhead.

Four or five guys could be in there talking with Bob Waters; A.B.C. would be in front of the mirror, turning this way and that, giving his complete attention to body and facial maintenance.

Not that others of us didn't do those things. I even tried trimming *my* armpit hair — the idea had never occurred to me before — but I always did it in my room when my roommate wasn't there. A.B.C. didn't care if you stood right beside him and watched him apply his skin lotion or ream out his ears or whatever. Some guys did talk to him while he was at the mirror — if you wanted to hold a conversation with him, you usually had to do it that way — and A.B.C. acted like of course, any sensible person would be interested in how he maintained his appearance.

We also pegged A.B.C. as a dummy. At the end of that first semester, though, when the rest of us on second floor Emmett were getting 2.0's and 1.8's, A.B.C. got a 3.5. We still thought he was a dumb jock narcissist, but we started using a more respectful tone when we talked about him behind his back. Also, there was his girl, Marcy; we met her when she came down for Midwinter's weekend.

Marcy hadn't yet finished high school, which was why she didn't show up in Charlottesville until second semester. Even though, according to A.B.C., her parents trusted him, they weren't letting their daughter make that trip until after she turned eighteen. Anybody could see why. All A.B.C. had told us about her was that she held the high school record for the city of Cleveland for the girls' 220-yard dash. Marcy was the girl every one of us was looking for. She was a tall, thin, Scandinavian blonde, with clear skin that made you want to brush her cheek with your fingertips, and eyes that were sometimes green and sometimes blue. I once even got into an argument with

Bob Waters over what color her eyes were, an argument that A.B.C. settled by informing us that her eyes changed according to what she was wearing. Marcy had seventeen or eighteen variations of a smile, a generous laugh, and a smart, teasing way of talking and looking us Emmett House guys in the eye. She made us happy we had peckers and wistful because it wasn't likely our peckers and Marcy were ever going to be acquainted. She was also restless and loose in the joints, so that when she was standing around talking to you, she seemed to be moving through a very subtle dance.

When I think back to that first time I met Marcy Bunkleman — at the little keg party we had in the lounge on the first floor of Emmett House — I can call up my exact sentiments: what atrocity of fate had allowed A.B.C. to claim this girl who'd been intended for me? There was no God.

Not that I and about a dozen others didn't try to get somewhere with Marcy. And that girl could flirt like she'd invented flirting. But it was like challenging a girl to a race and then finding out she's a world-class runner. No matter how fast you are, she's faster — lots faster. The first time I spoke to her was at our tacky little dorm party, with several cups of keg beer firing up my chromosomes. In those days I was known for being a master of chitchat, but my skills counted for nothing when it came to making an impression on this girl. In a matter of seconds it struck me that she was way ahead of me, was even being easy on me, coasting, so that I could catch up.

"So, Jimmy," she said. As she talked to me, she was moving this way and that in that dance of hers, and though I did think she was the coolest girl I'd ever met, it also occurred to me — briefly, I admit — that someone observing her from a distance might have thought she needed to pee. "Jimmy, you're saying the fraternities are the keepers of tradition here at U.Va., and you want to join one to make your contribution. How exactly do they do that? Do the guys all get together on Friday nights and study the history of U.Va.? Do they test the pledges on the U.Va. songs like that cute little wa-hoo-wa, gin-ee-ah you all were singing a minute ago?"

Out of the corner of my eye I noticed, to my left and behind me, A.B.C. — smirking. For all I knew, he was winking at Marcy over my shoulder while she talked with me. Flying through conversational sunlight with the girl I was born desiring, I had just experienced ecstasy; now, all of a sudden my face and neck were being blowtorched. As far as Marcy and A.B.C. were concerned, I was the entertainment of the afternoon.

Suffice it to say that A.B.C. and I became friends against my will. I never did like him, and I don't like him now, but we're friends, close friends. The average person can't understand that. The explanation for our friendship lies in the vicinity of Marcy. I married her best friend. I figured Uta was as close to Marcy as I was ever going to get.

Uta and I met not long after Boyce Patton broke my jaw for having, according to him, tried to snake his date at the Stan Kenton concert. Boyce was an unusually belligerent pal of A.B.C.'s, another baseball player, and I wouldn't have had the nerve to try to snake a date of his. When I struck up a friendly conversation with a brunette with a cheerful face standing in the lobby of Memorial Gymnasium during intermission, I wasn't aware she was Boyce Patton's date. Nor did I, when he walked up to the two of us just about the time I set my hand on that young lady's shoulder, in my immediate decisions about what to say and what to do, accurately assess Boyce's mood or alcoholic intake. What I got for my ten seconds of bad judgment was six weeks of having my lower jaw clamped to my upper jaw with wires and rubber bands.

Thus was I able to impress Uta Schildhaus with my reticence.
Had I been my normal, sociable self that spring, Uta would not
have found me attractive. It wasn't that I couldn't speak. By
shaping words with my cramped tongue and releasing them
through gritted teeth and puckered lips, I could make myself
understood, but I looked and sounded as if I were a hostile
person doing a Tweetie Bird imitation. Around strangers, especially women, it was better for me to be quiet. Mostly I was,
though of course I continued to desire the company of women
just as much as ever.

I couldn't pass up the Chi Phi Spring Formal Cocktail Recep-
tion. I knew A.B.C. had taken Marcy, and when I spotted them
in the crowd, I made my way over. Marcy was standing with an
equally tall and slightly more statuesque woman. This woman
had thrillingly high cheekbones, but she was a brunette, and I
was wary of dark-haired women. Neither Marcy nor A.B.C.
introduced us; it was too loud in there, and my oral condition
would have made an introduction all the more complicated.
She looked at me only once, a quick rake of her eyes down my
torso. I risked stepping closer. She didn't seem to mind my
standing right there beside her in the crowd. She was quiet. I
was quiet. We lingered in our capsule of space for a passage of
minutes, quietly sipping our gin-and-tonics, and maybe sway-
ing ever so slightly with each other, among all the chatting,
joking, shouting drinkers.

After a long while, Marcy and this woman excused themselves to go to the ladies'. I watched them make their way
through the crowd, long dark hair and long light hair, moving
in tandem. When they returned, Marcy whispered in my ear,
"Uta likes you."

The aftermath of that moment was an entire summer of
necking with Uta Schildhaus in those formal gardens between

the lawns and the ranges. Uta and Marcy were just entering nursing school at U.Va. A.B.C. was using summer school to try to get ahead in his language requirement at the same time that he was lifting weights and working on his swing with the batting coach. When I learned who was going to be where, I talked my parents into letting me enroll in a summer school language course, too; the same German class A.B.C. was taking, in fact. Only after the first day of class, when Herr Hummel called on each of us to read a paragraph from the text, did it occur to me that taking intermediate German with your mouth wired shut might be a problem.

Actually, it wasn't wired shut. The wires had been laced between my teeth to form rows of small hooks, top and bottom. Between the hooks were strung very short, sturdy rubber bands. I could stretch these bands slightly in order to take in the soup and the milkshakes with eggs in them that were my diet, and my doctor had given me some extra rubber bands in case I broke any of the ones he'd used to string me up. When Uta and I figured out we both liked to wait until after dark and then get close and slick with each other, like salamanders under a wet rock, I began popping bands out both sides of my mouth. I couldn't help it. One thing led to another, the way it does. She and I would find ourselves beginning a kiss as a peck on the lips and inexorably moving into a soul kiss that popped one of my bands and jolted both our heads. I unstrung myself to the point where I had to go back to the doctor for another examination and some more rubber bands.

Even though her silence was voluntary, Uta was just as isolated as I was, and, to put it bluntly, even though she'd had a strict Lutheran upbringing, she was just as horny as I was. Such a girl was an astonishment to me. Evenings, around dusk, she and I would meet at the Virginian, slog down some draft beer, listen to the jukebox, and carry out some friendly maneuvers beneath the table in our booth. We both knew when it was time for us to cruise onto the grounds and make our way up to the lawn; we'd tease each other as we walked by bumping hips and running our fingers down the insides of each other's arms. And then we'd meander back along the serpentine walls into Thomas Jefferson's Palladian gardens, find a bench in a dark corner under a magnolia tree, and commence Phase II, our please-don't-stop-now making-out.

Every night Uta wore a white brassiere; apparently her mother back in Cleveland thought white an absolute requirement for nursing students and had sent Uta down to Charlottesville with undergarments of no other color. By close to one A.M. — when she had to check into her dorm — Uta's brassiere and underpants would be in her skirt pocket, the crotch of my boxers would be soggy, and the two of us would go strolling back to McKim Hall, arm in arm, giggling, purring, and even moaning now and then, without having exchanged more than half a dozen complete sentences during the entire evening.

It wasn't so much that Uta didn't like to talk — she liked NOT talking. Very quickly, after I understood, I got behind her program. It was personal conviction; it was philosophy; it was living in the body.

A.B.C. teased me unmercifully about my broken-jawed German. "*Du bist ein Deutsche-sprecher mit kaput Zahler*" was the kind of thing he liked to say. "*Du machst ein grosse Scheissworten. Habst du ein Busenhalter in deiner Mund?*" A.B.C. was (and is) maybe the most excruciating buttocks-ache I personally have ever known, partly because he had Marcy, partly because he was certain his life was a success story that had already been written so that all he had to do was merrily live it out, and mostly because he had a natural talent for exasperating normal citizens like me. The worst thing about that whole summer was that he got into the habit of confiding in me all his views — personal, professional, foreign, national, and miscellaneous. It was like having somebody vomit in your ear several hours every day.

A.B.C. didn't believe in premarital sex, even though Marcy had told him she was interested. (That fact alone made me whimper aloud whenever he reminded me of it, and my little screams never failed to bring a smirk to his face.) A.B.C. thought he and Marcy would have no trouble staying faithful to each other if they waited for sex until they were married. The marriage, of course, in his long-range plan, was scheduled to take place the June after he graduated. A.B.C. thought guys like me, who were always trying to get laid, were the most ridiculous creatures on the face of the planet. "Right down there next to the baboons and the wart hogs," he liked to say. A.B.C. thought discipline should be cultivated in all areas of life. He himself did not drink more than one beer a night, did not smoke, did not eat dessert, did not stay up past midnight, and did not stick his tongue into any part of Marcy's body. "Look at you," A.B.C. said, "wasting all those rubber bands. Tell me, Rago, are you just *impelled* to get your tongue into Uta's mouth?"

"Not so," I said. It was my claim that Uta was the one who was *impelled* to get her tongue into my mouth and that was why I had had to go back to my surgical orthodontist. A.B.C. didn't believe me, but I didn't care. Denying whatever he said gave me more dignity than I would have had otherwise. Uta apparently talked a good deal to Marcy, though she did it out of my hearing, and Marcy apparently kept A.B.C. abreast of the latest developments in Uta's and my physical relationship. I hated A.B.C.'s knowing anything about my sex life, but it titillated me to know that Marcy was having to think about it.

There was a time when I was sure Uta had turned out to be a better wife for me than Marcy ever would have been. The fact that we didn't talk seemed to help us. Exchanging words wasn't how Uta and I communicated, though I am a verbal person. For years our bodies had things to say to each other, and I don't mean just sex. After we started actually having it, Uta and I never could get the flames turned up as high as they were that summer of everything-but.

And the thrill finally departed for Uta and me the way it does for everybody, after so many years and so many kids. For us, it wasn't so sad, though. When our older daughter started applying to college, Uta and I came to understand that we'd soon be looking straight into the leathery old face of grandparenthood. By that time, sex per se was not the first thought that came to our minds when we were alone in the house. But if I was cooking something in the kitchen, Uta would sometimes come in and stand beside me at the stove, and the two of us would stare into my skilletful of sautéing onions for a good and satisfying moment. Our shoulders might not even touch, but having her come and stand beside me like that was an exercise in emotional harmony. Or Uta might be sitting out on the deck, sipping coffee on a Saturday morning, and she'd call, "Hey, Jimmy, come out here." When I went out, she wouldn't say a word or even glance at me, but I'd know she wanted me to sit with her. It was hardly a thought. It'd just be what I wanted right then: to breathe the morning air in the company of my wife. Maybe a brown rabbit would slip out of the far tree line onto our lawn. Maybe the pair of male and female cardinals of our neighborhood would light down in our dwarf cherry tree the way they like to. Until our coffee got cold, Uta and I simply floated in the timestream.

I'm romanticizing the relationship; I know that. We fought,

we had our bad times — like everybody else or maybe worse. Uta came pretty close to leaving me the first time she was pregnant. Responsibility had an ugly face as far as I was concerned, so I'd put off becoming a father as long as I could. Then, when Uta wouldn't take no for an answer any longer and we got ourselves pregnant, I started acting like a frat boy. I went out to the bars, I grew a beard, I went back to my hometown and stayed with my parents for a week "to sort things out." That process somehow demanded that I call up Amy Spence, an old girlfriend from high school. After a night of drinking to the old times, Amy and I ended up in a motel. The next morning, when I saw who I was in the sack with, I commenced wailing, "Uta, Uta, Uta!" Amy Spence swore she wouldn't see me again even if she'd been through three more divorces by the next time I called her. And that wasn't the worst.

I came back to town, hung over and remorseful as an old basset hound, drove straight over to A.B.C.'s house, found Marcy out back, weeding the pansy bed, and confessed to her that I loved her, I'd always loved her, I wouldn't ever be able to love Uta or anybody else because of loving her. Even while the words were spilling out of my mouth, I knew I should be holding them back, but I'd lost control. Marcy flung her trowel at me and pelted me with topsoil until I had to retreat to my car. When I got back home, Uta had locked herself in our bedroom and wasn't about to come out. Marcy had called her and told her straight out what I'd said. I should have known that's how Marcy would handle it, no matter how much trouble it caused. She's not one to put up with deception.

A.B.C. came over to our house and tried counseling me — himself, personally. That was the thirteenth hall of hell. I dug my granddaddy's 12-gauge shotgun out of the closet and told A.B.C. that if he didn't get out of my living room, I was going out to shoot the tires off his car. I think Uta appreciated that, though she never said so. At least after I got A.B.C. out of the house that afternoon, Uta didn't seem to mind being in the same room with me anymore. And after I put us all through those antics, I lost my appetite for indulging my deeper urges. The pregnancy proceeded. Uta and I had our daughter, and all of a sudden there was plenty for both of us to do, a baby to hold our attention. Also, after Uta got her figure back, our bodies picked up their old enthusiasm for each other.

All of this is background, really, to what A.B.C. got himself into. A.B.C.'s always pretty much done what he wanted to. True, he made a lot of money as a lobbyist for one organization after another, but in his last phase he stopped doing anything so pedestrian as drive down to his office. A.B.C. journeyed out to the far edge. You wouldn't have thought it; at least I wouldn't have.

"Museum Man" was what Uta and I started calling him. For about a year, A.B.C. probably spent as many hours pacing the hallways of the National Gallery as he did in his own home. At U.Va. he'd minored in art history — one of his life axioms was "The successful man maintains a cultural awareness." It was laughable, really, and typical of A.B.C., like the Fuller Brush man studying Beethoven's symphonies in order to make small talk with his customers. But A.B.C. could take you to a museum and, without walking up to the identification card, tell you who painted which picture and the painter's birth and death dates and the title of his best-known picture.

"Vermeer is the guy who woke me up," A.B.C. explained. "Jan Vermeer, sixteen-thirty-two, sixteen-seventy-five. *The Girl with the Red Hat.* Always appealed to me because of her hat. Incredible scarlet aura spinning around her head like pure energy. Mouth open. Delicate coating of light that makes you think she's just licked her lips. Got to appreciate the composition. Lively and precise at the same time. The face of the girl isn't much, though. You like the look of her hat; you know it excites her to be wearing that hat. But there's nothing about the actual person. What she has to say wouldn't be much. Features are crude. Common girl all dressed up.

"Usually I spent all my time looking at that one painting, but this one day, instead of passing with a quick pause-and-look at the other paintings, the way I'd always done before — maybe because the room was empty, and I had plenty of time — I took one step closer to another of those Vermeers: *A Lady Writing*. One step closer to a picture I'd seen dozens of times before. Changed my life."

A.B.C. took me to see it the next week. The lady in the picture isn't really writing; she's stopped. Her pen — a small quill — is still in place on the paper, and her other hand is holding the page down. She's just looked up, as if you've interrupted her. Her face has this expression that's so warm and so complex — it's left over from the moment before she saw you. "Jimmy, you'd go nuts making up the story of this picture," A.B.C. said. "This lady is writing to her good friend — or maybe to her sister — about something that really pleases her. You wonder what it could be. You can almost sense the pleasure flying away from her as she stops her writing.

"*Look*, she says. *Go ahead and look. My life feels to me the same as yours feels to you — so full, I could burst. Please let me get back to my letter. You go on with whatever you were doing out there in the twentieth century.*"

Later on, when Marcy and I really could talk with each other, she told me that when A.B.C. came home that afternoon from his trip to the National Gallery and his one step closer to *A Lady Writing*, he tried to explain the experience to her while she was cooking dinner. Marcy wasn't a gourmet cook, but she took care when she prepared the food for her family. Even more than usual, A.B.C. that evening was on an undiscovered planet, talking, talking, talking. Wherever she moved in her kitchen, there he was, bumping into her, tripping her, and still yammering away about the picture. Finally Marcy asked him very politely to let her have ten minutes to get the meal together and she'd be pleased to hear about his trip while they ate.

He marched out of the kitchen. All through dinner, he talked as little as possible. Throughout the evening he stayed in Monosyllable City. Then, long after she'd gone to bed, he walked into their bedroom, woke her up, and informed her, "Marcy, I'm beginning to think we never should have gotten married."

Marcy said she could hear herself saying, in this sleepy voice, "A.B.C., let me get this straight. We've been married twenty-six years, we've had two kids, and you're saying we shouldn't have done it?" And A.B.C. said yes, and Marcy shut up. She didn't say aloud any of the obvious punch lines that kept occurring to her while A.B.C. waited for what else she had to say. She figured either he'd gotten himself worked up into a state that he'd pass through pretty quickly or else she was having a weird dream. Either way, it seemed like a good idea to roll over and do her best to go back to sleep.

But A.B.C.'s phase wasn't temporary. He kept going to the museums in search of "the one." It was a real woman he had in mind, even though he kept talking about "the one," as if it was a mystical concept of Western civilization. The one A.B.C. should have married, the one who was intended for A.B.C., the one with whom A.B.C. should have ascended to heaven. Et cetera. He didn't see the irony — the silliness, really — and he denied that there was any injustice to what he was doing.

"You know, Jimmy, you and Uta are my oldest friends. All these years, you guys are my witnesses. Do you know anybody who's ever been more committed to a spouse, a marriage, a family? You're looking at the original Mr. Monogamy." That was the spiel he gave me one night over at our house. It was almost eleven.

"You getting maybe a little bit tired, Mr. Monogamy?" I asked. "You feel like taking a rest?" I faked a yawn that, halfway through, turned into a real one.

"I'm not through yet, Jimmy! You just sit there and listen and try to do something different — learn something!" He wagged his finger at me. "You walk down the halls of the National Gallery. What's the picture you see most often, the picture that's painted in every century by painters of every nationality?"

I gave him another stifled yawn. "*Nude Descending a Staircase*," I said.

"See, Jimmy, you're going to learn something in spite of yourself. It's a picture of a female. *Portrait of a Lady. Girl Bathing. The Dancer. Madame Ginoux with Books. Mona Lisa.* What have you. Next question. What, by an overwhelming margin, is the gender of the painters who produced these pictures of females?"

"Gee, A.B.C., I couldn't begin to guess."

"Pardon my saying so, Jimmy, but when was the last time you wanted to sit and look at Uta the way you might want to sit and look at *A Montrouge* or *Woman Seated in Blue* or *The Lacemaker*? I mean, when I look at *The Lacemaker*, I want to sit down beside that young woman and hold the quietest, slowest conversation with her while she works. I want her to tell me her whole life from the first thing she can remember up to the moment she sat down to work on that piece of lace. I'll bet you every cent I've got that it's thirty years since you had even a little bit of curiosity about Uta and what her life's been like. I'm not trying to hurt your feelings, man. I'm just trying to wake you up."

"It's past my bedtime, A.B.C. I'm tired." I stood up and stretched.

"We're talking breakthrough here, Jimmy," he said, but at least he stood up, too. "Just being alert to the possibility that there's somebody out there who can break through to where you live."

"It's hard for me to get enthusiastic, A.B.C. Seems like a bad plan, driving in to Washington to look for women at the museum. You're looking in the wrong part of town, man."

I could tell he wanted to give me a sharp elbow to the ribs, but he didn't; instead, he forced himself to grin even wider. Then he gave me a soft punch on the shoulder and left. I was watching him walk down the steps of my front porch. I was thinking about Marcy hearing his car pull up in their driveway, listening to him unlock the door and come into the house. I was just about to close the door when A.B.C. turned back to me.

"I've decided to take myself seriously. That's all, Jimmy. And I can see how you might have a problem doing that, taking yourself seriously." He was using his old supercilious tone; it made me want to start heaving my furniture out at him. "Let me ask you a question, Jimmy." He paused significantly and waited to catch my eye. "How do you know this isn't what you're doing anyway, Jimmy? Looking for the one. Maybe you're carrying on your regular life, going to work, and coming home, and all those boring routines. But maybe there's this part of your consciousness that's staying alert, casting an eye this way and that way wherever you go, hoping you're finally going to see her."

"Sure, maybe so, A.B.C. No question, it's a possibility. Good night now."

I had my hand back on the door when he said, "You should probably also consider whether or not Uta might be keeping an eye out, too."

"Drive carefully, A.B.C.," I said. Son of a bitch thought he could ruffle my feathers, but he couldn't. He wasn't telling me anything I hadn't thought of before — plenty of times. I locked the doors, went up to our bedroom, and slipped in beside Uta, who was either asleep or faking it; either way, I didn't want to bother her. And pretty soon I was either asleep or faking it, too; I couldn't tell which.

Next morning I still had A.B.C. with me, whispering his suggestions into my mind's ear while I fixed Uta's breakfast tray. I took care to make her toast and coffee just so. It was important for her to get the right kind of start to her day, because her job was so stressful — she was the district supervisor for intensive-care nurseries in northern Virginia. In her area of responsibility, Uta usually had at least a dozen babies — and sometimes those tiny creatures were closer to protoplasm than babies — hovering between life and death. She knew she shouldn't, but she felt personally responsible for keeping all those microscopic pulses beating. One day she told me her job had taught her more about God than all her years of growing up in the Lutheran Church. Because she could bear that stress and responsibility, Uta was also the one who brought in the money for us. I did a little teaching at the community college in town and some free-lance journalism, but the fact of the matter was — I don't mind admitting it — I was a house-husband. It's the way things evolved in our marriage, but it was also — I admit this, too — more or less the way I chose for them to evolve.

I looked forward to those little intersections of mood that

enabled Uta and me to carry out bits of verbal communication
— like three-minute newscasts. One of them was when Uta was
just waking up on a weekday. I'm a morning person. I want to
get my hands on the newspaper as soon as the paperboy flings
it onto the porch, and I want to have my coffee ready even
before the newspaper's arrived. But Uta liked to ease herself
slowly into the day. So I'd bring her breakfast on a tray, along
with the paper, which I'd already read all the way through to the
classified ads. Usually I had suggestions about which articles
would be of interest to her. I'd hang out in our bedroom with
her for a chat while she sat up in bed and got herself going.
Sometimes I thought I could actually see Uta putting her brain
in gear when she got the pillows arranged behind her and
reached for the paper. That particular morning I'd brought up
my own cup of coffee (my fourth), because I expected Uta
would have some stimulating observations when I told her
about A.B.C. going national with his quest.

"Such a silly idea. Such a silly man," she said. She had the
faintest curl of a smile on her lips. Her hair was out of kilter in
several ways, and her face was puffy from sleep and a little
flushed from waking up. Her eyelids drooped ever so slightly.
Her cheekbones shone a little, as if they'd been polished by the
pillow she'd slept on. It was a way that only the girls and I had
ever seen her, a way that would have embarrassed her if I'd
called her attention to it, but when she looked like that, I experienced little jolts of affection for her. "How long did you let
him go on talking, Jimmy?" she asked, by which I knew she
meant to chide me for not turning him out earlier and coming
to bed before she fell asleep.

Uta sipped her coffee, her eyes directed toward the front page
of the paper. I stood at the window and watched my neighbor
set out his trash. "How do you suppose he goes about it?" she

asked. "He walks into the museum. There are people all around him. Does he hold interviews?"

I was charmed by her questions. "He goes to rooms where they have the paintings he likes," I answered. "I don't know why I think this is what he does, but it's how I see him doing it. Usually they have these places where you can sit in the middle of the room. I think he sits down near a painting he admires and watches the people who come to see it. 'You can tell a lot by how a person stands in front of a painting.' Didn't he say that the other night?"

Uta gave the newspaper a sleepy grin, as if to say, How do I know what he says? I turned back to the window, but there was nothing of interest out there. I'd started for the stairs when Uta startled me.

"How do you do," she said, faking a man's voice. "I'm Allen Ballston Crandall, also known as A.B.C. What's your name?" From the bed, she extended her hand toward me.

"How do you do," I said, taking her hand and solemnly shaking it. "My name is Angela Bagnoli."

Uta clasped my hand with both of hers and pulled me toward her. "Come here, Angela. I'm holding interviews with young women like yourself to see if you are THE ONE. Come right into this bed, please. This is where I interview my candidates. Oh, by the way, you have to take off your clothes. Did I explain that to you? Oh, yes, well that's just how I do it. I take mine off, too, so we're all even, no? Yes, of course, certainly."

Sometimes I thought Uta could be a real talker if she'd just let herself go. But later, when we'd made her late for work and she was hurrying to shower and dress and get out of the house, she hardly had a word to say to me. It didn't matter, of course, because that's what I was used to. But still, when she had a little burst of language like that, I wondered how it would have been if I'd married somebody who was really verbal, the way I am. On the other hand, Marcy married A.B.C., and they were both talkers, though he didn't ever listen to her. In all those years of knowing them, I'd never seen him pay any attention to what Marcy said. When the four of us were together, A.B.C. would pontificate, more or less in Uta's direction, and Marcy and I would talk quietly to each other, holding a kind of sotto voce conversation underneath all the verbiage A.B.C. was generating. And with expressions moving across her face like cloud shadows on a windy field, Uta would sit still, staring at her fingernails. For years, it was that way with the four of us.

That morning the house was empty and quiet. It was Monday, my day to do the laundry, though with the girls out of the house, I figured that Uta and I could go another week or even two and still have plenty of clean clothes. Nevertheless, if you don't want your life to disintegrate, you can't let your laundry day pass by. I was down in the basement, checking out the whites for stains, with the darks turning in the dryer and the pastels sloshing in the washer, when all of a sudden somebody about a foot behind me shouted, "Jimmy!"

I leaped, I hollered, I wrenched my body backward. Marcy Crandall, née Bunkleman, the beloved of my life, in blue jeans and a T-shirt that said DANCE THROUGH THE APOCALYPSE, faced me, a look of horror on her face. "I rang the doorbell," she said. She was still shouting, but she was also clutching at my hands to calm me down. "I came in and yelled as loud as I could. I'm really sorry, Jimmy. I didn't mean to scare you."

If I'd thought I could have got away with it, I'd have denied I was scared. Sure, I was startled, but I was also out-and-out flabbergasted that she was here at all. Yet here she was — and wearing a face so full of anxiety and apology for what she'd done to me that I could hardly stand it. "That's okay, Marcy," I said. "Anybody can benefit from facing certain death at the hands of the Laundry Room Serial Killer. Let's go upstairs and get some coffee."

I led the way. In my tender condition, I did not want to follow Marcy's derrière up our narrow basement staircase. At the moment it seemed passing strange to me that I had desired an unavailable woman through her twenties, her thirties, and her forties, through her having two kids and raising them, and through her long marriage to somebody else. Surely I didn't lust for her anymore. I mean, I definitely had these yearnings for her, but I didn't have a real name for what we were. Not-lovers, I guess — the lovers of knots. Marcy and I had been knot-lovers for almost thirty years.

She'd never gained weight. Even when she was pregnant, she looked like a skinny pregnant woman. She probably weighed about what she did the first time I met her, but her body had definitely become more reasonable than it was when she was eighteen. And her hair had picked up some character from that shimmering Mary-of-Peter-Paul-and-Mary gold that it used to be; some of it had gone white and some of it had grown darker. Also, that jittery way she had of moving around when she was standing up had disappeared. Marcy Bunkleman, the former Cleveland champion high school sprinter, could finally stand still. What a sad comment that was on my generation.

I busied myself with making a fresh pot of coffee while she sat on the kitchen stool. She wasn't talking, and it occurred to me right then that she probably should be telling me what she was doing over at my house. Marcy had never sought my company, never wanted to be with just me by myself. She'd never given me any excuse to make a pass at her. When Uta and I were over at their house or they were over here, Marcy had avoided

being stranded in a room with me. I was grateful to her; at least
I'd never been able to think that maybe she secretly pined for
me. "So how come you're over here this morning, Marcy?" I
murmured.

Blunt as it was, my question didn't provoke an answer right
away. I began to feel silly for having asked it, and I turned from
the coffee maker to her. Apparently she'd found something so
fascinating in the pattern of the kitchen floor linoleum that her
complete attention was required. Then her eyes snapped up to
meet mine, and we were like kids in a staring contest.

"Uta told me I should talk to you," she said. I waited. We kept
staring. It's funny about looking into somebody's face. I guess if
you've just fallen in love with somebody, you'd want to do that
a lot. But I'll swear, if you scrutinize it objectively, nobody's face
is beautiful. Little moles and blotches and flakes and blackheads
and pimples become apparent, not to mention the utter weird-
ness of the features of the human face and their arrangement.
You start remembering that our eyes are placed in the front of
our skulls because we're predators, and so on. This is a line of
thought you don't necessarily want to practice with your beloved. It's like thinking too carefully about a single word; if you
go far enough, you can't believe that a word actually means
what it's supposed to mean. Cauliflower, cello, clock, coffee — I
mean, you can disassemble the entire English language if you
get to studying it word by word. So there I was, looking at
Marcy's face and not wanting to see her that way, every line at
the corner of her mouth and the bruised little pockets beneath
her eyes. "So talk," I whispered to her.

"I want you to tell me what you think . . ." she whispered
back to me; then she shook her head and said out loud, "about
A.B.C. and his fucking museums." When she got to "fucking
museums," she was hitting the counter with the side of her fist.

The spell, whatever it was that had me looking too closely into her face and whispering to her in my kitchen, was broken. It was all right now. I'd been needing exactly that, to see Marcy mad as a teased alligator over what A.B.C. was up to. All of a sudden I felt serene; I was a monk perched on a rock ledge high in the Himalayas; up there it was only me and the great snowy mountaintops; below, in the far distance, lay the valley of petty human affairs. "All right," I said. "I can tell you about A.B.C. and his museums, Marcy. I am well suited to do exactly this for you." And so I made it up for her.

Probably right now — what is it, 9:25? — A.B.C. is coming off Route 66 onto Constitution Avenue. Is he thinking about women? Yes. The part of his mind that isn't thinking about parking spaces is thinking about women, but in the abstract.

It's going to be warm today. The tourists are in shorts and T-shirts, but they're not holding A.B.C.'s attention. Aside from the ones who go once every five years with their husbands and kids, women who go to museums are not your cross section of American females, especially the ones who go there on weekday mornings. A.B.C. shakes his head over these women. Got to work up a profile sometime, he thinks. Average number of years of education — seventeen; average amount of money spent on clothes being worn to the museum that day — four hundred dollars. Average number of languages spoken — three. They're either totally out of the question, or else they're real candidates. Dogs or angels, he thinks; nobody in between. He figures the right one is looking, too, though she may not know it or be willing to admit it to herself. A.B.C. figures it's going to be a woman by herself. Probably one of those with three or four languages, a graduate degree, and five hundred dollars worth of clothes on her back. That's how he flatters himself. He's also wearing jacket and tie; he looks sharp enough that somebody with an eye for that kind of thing would probably peg him as a U.Va. grad. Fifty years old, and he's still buying clothes at Eljo's.

The doors open. A.B.C. steps inside. He's taken off his blazer in the sunshine, but now it's cool enough for him to put it back on. He walks upstairs to the rotunda, with the statue of Mercury and the fountain. It's cool and dark up there. He heads to the right, down the main corridor. Suddenly the place is populated. A.B.C. shakes his head. From all over the world people come here to look at pictures. Once, A.B.C. was one of them, a picture-looker. Now he hardly pays any attention to the paintings. He shakes his head over that, too, and decides to pay a visit to his old and valued acquaintances, the three Vermeer paintings.

But A.B.C. has managed to put himself into a trance by looking at the faces of the people around him. The women, of course, he knows he's supposed to be studying; he's paying attention, though, to the other faces, too: the men, the children, the old ladies, the faces of the guards. For some reason, he can't let one person walk past without having a look. Something's making him do it. Never going to find her like this, he thinks, and tries to shake his head at himself.

Even on the best of days, the National Gallery is kind of disorienting. Today A.B.C. can't navigate. He's not really lost, but he damn sure can't find the room with the Vermeers. These rooms are so much alike, and of course there are no windows, just walls full of paintings. He stands stock-still for a moment, but the faces are relentless. He wants to put his hands over his face. He wants to smooth down his eyelids with his fingertips.

A.B.C. forces himself to find his way outside. Once the fresh air hits him and he gets his tie undone, he feels a little better. He's standing more or less by himself. He finds himself walking down the stone steps from the gallery's main entrance; he's headed toward a woman sitting under a tree, fanning herself with a bro-

chure. He walks through the stopped line of cars and goes up to her.

She is Ardelia Schrieble, born in 1947, from Flint Hill, Virginia, wearing sunglasses right now. She doesn't like being in Washington or any other city, but she's here today visiting her son and daughter-in-law, who are inside the museum, looking at pictures, while Ardelia is taking a break out here. Ardelia has never before visited the National Gallery, and she didn't like it in there. She still hasn't got herself quite together. The man who's approached her, with his jacket over his shoulder, looks ordinary enough, which is why she wasn't afraid when she noticed him walking toward her. But now he's just standing here, looking at her, and Ardelia doesn't like it. Clumsy in her hurry, she picks herself and her pocketbook up from this grassy place under the tree that had looked so inviting a few minutes ago. "What are you staring at?" she hears herself saying in too shrill a voice. She moves toward the museum, looking over her shoulder as she goes. Yes, he's following her. The man is following her. "I need you to take off your sunglasses, Miss," he's calling to her. "Miss!" he calls. "Miss! Miss!"

At first Marcy's face had that awful, hurt look. But what came out of her after a moment was laughter, the old unabashed laughter that I'd known from when she was eighteen and I was nineteen. And I was laughing with her — at A.B.C.'s expense, but that was all right with both us. It was fine for him to pay for Marcy and me having a laugh together. He could afford it.

"Did you see that, Jimmy?" Marcy asked. "Did you really see that?"

"You're damn right I saw it." I was shameless in swearing that to her because I knew we both needed what I'd said to be the truth. So we went on chuckling for a short moment. And then Marcy caught my eye. I couldn't help seeing how tired she was, how dark the thin puffy skin under her eyes was and how she'd put on a little eye make-up but had rushed the job or hadn't cared whether she got it right. Though I could hardly believe the treachery of my feelings, I wanted to look away. It was the first time in all my years of knowing Marcy that I'd wanted not to look at her.

"Come here, Jimmy," she said. I was scared of what she was going to do. I was even thinking of blurting out, "I don't think I want you anymore, Marcy." It was too late. She stood up, took my arms and set them around her shoulders, put her arms around my waist, and was squeezing me hard against her. The whole front of her body was pressed against the whole front of my body. I was thinking that the gods were nothing if not sadists for letting it happen that way.

"So now, Jimmy, we're really friends," Marcy said.

For the moment I didn't have anything to say. I felt as if I'd need about an hour to process my last thirty seconds of experience.

"This is a friendly hug?" I said.

"This is a friendly hug," Marcy said. At the moment, her breasts were so definitely and so intimately pressing against my chest — even her pelvis was just so profoundly there against my pelvis — that I almost felt that she and I were about to start making out. But Marcy wasn't aroused, and I wasn't, either.

"I've got to go, Jimmy." She squeezed me once more and let me go.

Whoosh, she'd gathered up her car keys and her sunglasses and was out the front door. Without much thought as to what I was up to, I found myself heading downstairs to the basement. Apparently some part of my consciousness had vague plans for me to busy myself with the laundry. My theory is that next to going on a safari and shooting a lot of wild animals, there's nothing like doing several loads of laundry to clear a man's mind. That morning, I confess that I took unusual pleasure in folding the clothes that came out warm from the dryer.

Finally the dryer and the washing machine were into their cycles again and the clean stuff was all folded and arranged in the basket. I walked upstairs. Just as I was stepping into the main hallway, there was Uta, coming in the front door. Because I'd been down in the basement, the blast of sunlight behind her momentarily blinded me. Uta didn't say hello, and neither did I. This is how we were. The thought scuttled across my brain that, dropping by for lunch like that, Uta could have stepped into the kitchen while Marcy and I were trying out our friendly hug. That would have put some pepper in the soup.

When I got my daylight vision, Uta had come all the way up to me, and I was looking her right in the face. I was studying her nose, which was by no means a cute little turned-up job but was most definitely a nose of character. I was seeing how the two slightly raised lines of flesh jutting down from her nose to her lips rather elegantly complemented the indented lines that angled down and away to either side of her mouth. All of a sudden I was having myself a moment. In her face, I was seeing back through the Utas I had known all those years of living with her and even back through the Utas who were around before I'd met her, a young girl, a still younger girl, a little girl. I saw all the way back to the face of Uta the baby! I didn't know how such a thing could happen. Every one of those faces was right there in Uta's face while I was looking at her.

Another corridor of time opened up in the opposite direction. Utas I was going to see in the years to come showed themselves to me, too, one after another, like a slide show on fast forward. I had to blink and blink from all I was being permitted to see. When the moment closed down, I was aware of exhaling. Apparently seeing several hundred faces of your wife backward and forward in time can make you hold your breath. There was only one Uta looking back at me right then, checking me out as I stopped blinking and my breathing returned to normal. I checked her out, too. This one had an arched eyebrow and about nine percent of a smile for me.

"Hello, Uta," I said.

4

The Story of a Million Years

IF HE COULD, Jimmy would have been unfaithful to me. He couldn't seem to manage it. Jimmy was incorrigibly domestic, which always made him very dear to me. I imagine that he felt terrible for what he thought of as his various infidelities. It was true that now and then he made a ruckus of unfaithfulness — there was the time he confessed his long-time love to Marcy, my best friend. But being a rake is only what Jimmy thought he wanted to be. The truth was that he wanted to be what he was, a house-husband — Mr. Stay-at-Home-and-Tend-to-Things.

When Jimmy and I got married, I was the one who brought in most of the income; a good nurse earns a pretty good salary. I was also the one who paid the bills, the one who decided when to get a new car, and so on. Jimmy taught part-time at the community college, and he did some free-lance journalism, but what he mostly did, in addition to spending time with our girls, was shop, cook, clean house, and do the laundry.

When Jimmy was a kid, he helped take care of a younger sister, Edna, who died of leukemia — and he never got over wanting to take care of people. Long before he thought about getting married, long before he met me, Jimmy was a husband.

I fell in love with him and married him for that married quality. I knew him better than he would ever know himself. I even knew better than to explain to him some of the things I knew — such as why he spent so much time listening to A.B.C.'s crazy ideas.

Marcy and I had known A.B.C. since we were all in high school. He was almost like part of our childhood. Jimmy was in A.B.C.'s first-year dormitory at U.Va. After he came into the picture, Marcy and I could never quite figure out whether he was closer to me or to A.B.C. Jimmy always told me how much he couldn't stand A.B.C., how despicable A.B.C.'s behavior was, and so on. Not only does A.B.C. do most of what he wants to do whenever he wants to do it, he also wants to be loved for being that way. Don't ask me why. Women don't want to move through their lives the way men do, pushing through a crowd of people to get where they think they should be. Jimmy isn't like that, which is probably why A.B.C. was so fascinating to him.

One night, A.B.C. told Marcy, Jimmy, and me this dream he'd had. It was a disturbing dream, and he wanted us to help him figure out what it meant. It wasn't exactly a dream of flying, because there was some kind of transportation to which he was connected, as if he were strapped to the nose of a plane, the prow of a ship, the engine of a train. Whatever it was that propelled him forward he couldn't really see. The speed wasn't the primary thing in the dream. Instead, it was his mastery of space; the way he passed through the mountains and cities and river valleys. The landscape was like an instrument that he could play as his mood inspired him.

"It was a very good dream up to that point," A.B.C. purred in that sly way that always makes me want to give him a quick smack across his face. But then, he said, the dream changed. He had less and less control of both the speed and the direction.

Finally, whatever it was that had picked him up, that had given him this incredible ride, raised him to a great height above the earth and then sent him careening downward at an insane velocity. A.B.C. hit the earth with a devastating impact. And he saw that he wasn't harmed at all. He remembered thinking, "How come I'm not dead yet?"

"It's a little boy's dream, A.B.C.," I told him, but he ignored me. Or he acted like he was ignoring me. I know he paid attention to what I said, mostly because I never said much around him. Jimmy sat forward in his chair. I could tell he didn't quite understand the dream, but he knew he liked it; it connected to something inside him. He asked A.B.C. questions. Long after Marcy and I had gone to the kitchen to fix some tea for ourselves, he and A.B.C. were still talking about the silly dream.

But, like Jimmy, I wasn't always in touch with all my feelings about the man. A few years ago, Jimmy and I drove down to Key West with the Crandalls for a vacation in March. We left all our kids with a sitter over at Marcy and A.B.C.'s house. When we were in college, we never took any of those road trips everybody else took at spring break. Back then, A.B.C. was playing baseball for U.Va., so he wasn't able to go. Marcy and I and Jimmy usually ended up hanging around Charlottesville, pretending to study. So this trip was going to be a spring break for grown-ups. On the drive down we were all four really enjoying ourselves, singing along with the radio, stopping to eat at these corny little roadside places left over from the fifties.

Wouldn't you know something would go wrong? When we got to the motel, we called home and found out that three of our four kids had come down with the flu. It was serious stuff that year; they were calling it the California flu, because a couple of children out there had actually died from it — high fevers, throwing up, complete exhaustion, all that. So we checked out of the motel an hour after we'd checked in and put Jimmy and Marcy — the main kid-raising parent from each family — on a plane back to Dulles. A.B.C. and I started driving the car north. No big deal; we've all known each other forever, and we all know that I have a low tolerance for A.B.C.'s ways. "Uta doesn't go for A.B.C.'s bullshit" is what Jimmy loves to tell people when he's talking about his hero.

Driving up through Florida, A.B.C. and I don't have much to say to each other. Even though it's my car, A.B.C. is at the wheel. I didn't feel like arguing with him when he asked for the keys, but it did start me out in a nasty frame of mind. We're both pissed that our vacation is ruined, the weather is hot, and all we've got to look forward to is miles and miles of interstate.

After we cross up into Georgia, the weather cools down, and I realize we've been driving in almost complete silence. "Put a little music into this show, Allen," I say. I turn on the car radio and tune in a station. A.B.C. gives me a feeble grin, like he also wishes we were having a better time but doesn't have very high hopes for it.

All of a sudden this radio station is playing Ray Charles tunes from back in the sixties, "What'd I Say?" and "I Got a Woman" and "Hit the Road, Jack." It's crazy, but a long time ago, at mixers or frat parties or wherever a Ray Charles song would come along, if there was dancing to be done, A.B.C. would find me or I would find him, and we'd dance like nothing you've ever seen — muscles straining, sweat flying, and get out of our way, please, everybody, can't you see we need every bit of this space? When the song was over, I'd be blushing like I'd just had sex with the man out there on the floor. I'd see people gaping at us as we walked off the dance floor, and that would make me blush all the more. The way we danced sometimes, it was pretty close to having sex with our clothes on. In just about every other way, he and I had no use for each other. But to that music, I had to dance with A.B.C., and he had to dance with me. I know he's vain, I know he can't think about anybody but himself. I hate all those things about him — except when Ray Charles starts singing and I need the right man to dance with. Marcy and Jimmy kidded each other and us about it, but we knew they didn't like it. A.B.C. and I didn't blame them.

So we're driving up the interstate, the weather's finally turned nice, and we're listening to Ray doing "You Are My Sunshine" in that way that turns on A.B.C. and me every time we hear it. He looks over at me and winks. I look back at him and raise my eyebrows. We're bopping our heads, sliding our shoulders, and snapping our fingers. We're a couple of kids out on the road with nothing but good times coming to us. It's bad; I know it is. I need to tell him, "Don't be thinking whatever it is you're thinking, A.B.C.," but I don't. The thrill doesn't come to me so much anymore. This afternoon I haven't gone looking for it, but now that it's here, along with a cool wind in my hair and Mr. Ray Charles giving us the song, I'm not going to turn it off. I glance over at A.B.C. and push the hair out of my eyes.

A.B.C. and I eat lunch at the Peach Pit Bar-B-Q in northern Georgia. Things are different between us. He's asking me questions, and I'm answering him. I'm enjoying answering him. He says he's amazed to find out that I can actually speak more than a couple of sentences at a time. It's true, I don't have much to say in most circumstances, especially social occasions — and especially to him. I've always had lots to say to Marcy, and every now and then Jimmy finds a way to get me talking. "I actually like talking, you know," I tell him. "It's just that you've never shown any interest in what I might have to say."

"Not true, U.! Not true at all." But he's grinning when he says it, and I know he knows it's so true.

"You think Marcy and Jimmy would rather be home taking care of our sick kids or sitting here stuffing their faces with barbecue and cole slaw like us?" he asks me.

"This is a cruel thing to say," I answer, "but I'll swear, I think they'd rather be home. Both of them."

A.B.C. nods solemnly, but it's not more than a couple of seconds before he and I are grinning at each other and moaning about how full we are as we stand up and head for the cashier's counter.

So there's a little buzz in the air between us as we're moving up through South Carolina. A.B.C. has given me the wheel — which is almost beyond remarkable; so far as I know, he's never let Marcy drive him anywhere, in his car or hers. We've taken the western corridor toward home, Interstate 77, and as we come up into North Carolina, the sky is looking pretty strange way up ahead of us. A.B.C. nods at it and looks at me. I shrug.

An hour later, we're in a blizzard. In one day we've gone from weather that would have let us swim and sunbathe on the beach in Florida, to slick roads and low visibility in the mountains of western North Carolina. "What the fuck?" A.B.C. shouts at the windshield. I think it's just about the same question I've got on my mind. A Mayflower moving van passes us, blinds us, and nearly blows us off the road.

So A.B.C. and I sit in the parking lot of the Holiday Inn just outside Mount Airy, North Carolina, and the topic of discussion is one room or two. It's not an argument, and we're not mad at each other. Crazy as it is, we're trying to figure how to play it for Jimmy and Marcy. A.B.C. says it doesn't make any difference to him, but I'm guessing he doesn't want to be alone, either. Something about the snow: coming down like this in the springtime, it's scary.

I make the decision: two rooms. They give us two next to each other on the ground floor. I unpack what I need. Then — so we don't have to make separate calls — I go to A.B.C.'s room and dial the Crandalls' number at home to tell them what's what and find out how things are there. There's a light snow in the D.C. area, so the crazy blizzard in North Carolina makes sense to them. Marcy's on the phone in Jenny's room, where the girls are holed up in their sickbeds, and Jimmy's on the phone downstairs in the kitchen. He's on his way back to our house. I don't like talking on the phone to the two of them, so I put A.B.C. on the line and listen to him taking pains to let them know we've taken two rooms. They go on telling him about the girls, who are definitely sick as dogs but who don't seem likely to die. They exchange good-byes, take-cares, and see-you-tomorrows.

When he sets the receiver down, A.B.C. and I are sitting opposite each other on the beds with the little bedside phone cabinet between us. I sit there, and he sits there. I can't bring myself to look him in the eye. I don't think he's looking straight at me, either. This moment goes on too long before A.B.C. finally says, "Dinner, U."

"Dinner, Allen," I say, too. I sound like a zombie. "Zombie dinner," I say. When A.B.C. asks me what the hell I'm talking about, I shake my head and make a little grimace. I don't bother changing clothes. While A.B.C. brushes his teeth, I sit in my zombie pose, and of course I can't help thinking about Marcy.

She had a secret that always intrigued me, and I never understood why she wanted it to be a secret: she taught herself to play the piano, and she did it on the old piano at my house. Marcy didn't take lessons. She was on the track team. From grade school on, she had been this champion runner, so she never had time for piano lessons or anything else after school. But good girl that I was in those days — fifth or sixth grade, I guess, was when I started — I took lessons once a week and had all the workbooks and everything. I was such a totally average piano student that my parents used to ask me to shut the door to the rec room downstairs when I practiced. They wanted to hear me just enough to know they weren't wasting their money on those lessons, but they didn't want to have to really listen to the dreadful things I did to music in my practice sessions.

Marcy and I had always hung out at each other's houses on weekends. When I started taking piano, she and I would tramp down the steps to the basement, and I'd show off for her what I'd learned. She was a great audience, because she stood right beside me and paid careful attention to what I told her and what I was doing. I felt very important, explaining all the piano rules to her — like how you're supposed to sit and hold your hands and touch the keys. One Saturday afternoon when I was struggling through "Little Brown Jug," she tapped me on the shoulder. "I don't think that's right," she said.

"Yeah?" I said. "Well, let me hear you play it the right way."

I stood up, thinking she'd say something like, "Oh, no, Uta, I can't play. You're the one taking lessons." She said nothing, and she was quick to take my place on the piano stool. She squinted at the music in front of her and checked out her hands on the keys — I'd shown her, the week before, how you're supposed to line yourself up with middle C. Then she played through the piece without any mistakes that I could hear — and picked up the tempo as she went. When she finished, she put her hands in her lap and stared at the practice book in front of her.

"How did you do that?" I asked.

"I don't know," she murmured. When she turned to face me, she had this very distressed expression on her face.

Without actually ever verbalizing it, we worked out a deal. Marcy would help me with the pieces I was supposed to be practicing, and that kept me in my teacher's good graces. In fact, she was the one who spent most of the time sitting at the piano. She was the one learning to play. I preferred lolling away the time over on the old sofa down there, watching TV with the sound turned all way down so my parents wouldn't hear. They never had a clue, which I guess is testimony to how little attention they were paying me in those days.

"That sounds wonderful, my darling," my mother would chirp when we stomped up the stairs for snacks or whatever. It soon became clear that she'd been hearing only the basic piano noise from downstairs; she'd given no thought to what the music was or which one of us might have been playing it.

As far as I know, I am the only person, besides herself, who knows that Marcy Bunkleman was a self-taught prodigy pianist.

Why didn't she want anybody to know what she was up to?

There was a fall Saturday afternoon, in our eighth-grade year, when she and I were out on my back porch — which wasn't the place I really wanted to be with Marcy, because all my parents had out there was an ordinary back yard, whereas behind their house the Bunklemans had a swimming pool and patio. It got unusually hot that day, so Marcy and I made iced tea and settled ourselves into opposite corners of the squeaky old glider. We were being pissy with each other, the way you can be with people who've been your friends forever. We were even jostling our feet and shins against each other's in a kind of mock fighting. I knew Marcy had come over to my house mostly because she wanted to play our piano. "I don't feel like going down there just yet," I said, watching her face to gauge how much I was irritating her. "Why do you want to go down in such a dark place when we can sit out here in the sun?" To make it harder on her, I tried to use a parental tone of voice.

In my meanness I even went so far as to say that I was thinking about telling my parents I wanted to quit taking piano lessons. Until that very moment, I'd done no such thinking, but when I saw how desperate Marcy was to maneuver me into not quitting, I began to understand what power I had over her. In the mood I was in that afternoon, I enjoyed having her at my mercy. She stopped jostling me, moved over into her corner of the glider, facing away from me, and was quiet for some moments.

"What difference does it make to you?" I nagged. I wanted her to have to say something. I wanted her to have to beg me for what I intended to give her anyway. I really was just teasing, because the truth was I loved those times of being with her down in our basement. I even liked the way she and I were bamboozling the adults, keeping it a secret from her parents that she could play and tricking my parents into thinking I was making such great progress.

When she turned to me, I saw that her face was pale. The pain I was causing her was monstrous, though I'd intended only a little pinprick. "You're the most hateful person I know," she whispered. She stood up and walked inside. Because I was so certain that she'd wait for me in the kitchen or the living room, I sat still for a minute or so before I followed her in. By then, she had gathered up her things and started walking back home.

I never heard her play again. It's been years since I thought about that old trouble between Marcy and me, and remembering it now makes it feel even stranger to be stuck in this motel with her husband. It's like a bad dream, walking with A.B.C. down the corridor toward the dining room.

The Holiday Inn serves us up a dinner fit for zombies. I can't imagine what I was thinking to have ordered the seafood stir-fry, which is greasy and tasteless; on the other hand, I can't imagine anything on this menu that I would have liked. A.B.C. doesn't finish his beef tournedos, which means they must be gruesome. We don't talk about it, though; the unaccept-able food is merely a depressing understanding between us. Through the floor-to-ceiling restaurant windows we watch the snow floating down; they've got spotlights on outside, so the huge flakes look like swarms of monster moths swirling against a black background. It's the third week of March, nearly cherry blossom time in D.C.

"What time is it?" I ask A.B.C.

"Quarter of eight." His voice has this amused and exhausted and exasperated and slightly curious tone. I understand him. When we were roommates in nursing school, Marcy used to say that I didn't know nearly as much about what people were thinking as I thought I did. What she didn't understand was that quiet people learn to pay attention to things like some-body's tone of voice. In this case, A.B.C. is telling me what time it is, but he's actually asking, "Isn't this a hell of a mess?" and, "What are we going to do with all these hours ahead of us?"

"Let's do dessert," I say. "Holiday Inn has decent desserts."

"What idiot told you that, U.? Holiday Inn is the enemy of every variety and nationality of food. Holiday Inn has decent nothing whatsoever, except maybe forks and spoons."

So we order the brownie à la mode for him, the carrot cake for me. They're edible, which cheers us a bit. Over the decaf, we're leaning back in our chairs, taking stock, looking at the other diners, who are glancing back at us. A.B.C. says they're figuring us for a married couple. He's right; it's evident from the way they let their eyes skim across us, checking us off their nothing-remarkable-there lists. Or maybe that's the way I'm seeing all the other couples in there. There's nobody in the whole dining room who looks like anyone I'd want to talk to for longer than about three minutes.

"Did Marcy ever tell you what happened to me that time I went to New York?"

A.B.C. shakes his head and looks at least half interested. Something makes me want to tell him the story, so I go ahead with it. It was spring break in Marcy's and my senior year of nursing school. Jimmy's parents had made him come home to help paint the family's summer place. Marcy hadn't wanted to leave Charlottesville, and I was sick of hanging out down there. So on a last-minute whim, I'd gone to New York with a couple of friends, Nancy Parks and Margaret Atwater. They were classmates of ours, girls we liked but didn't know all that well. The price Marcy and I paid for being such good friends with each other was that we didn't develop really close friendships with other girls. Nancy and Margaret were the same way, close to each other but more like friendly acquaintances with everybody else. Both pairs of friends appreciated each other even if we weren't all that intimate. Nancy and Margaret knew these guys from high school who had an apartment in the city and would let us sleep on the floor and the sofa of their living room.

I'd never been to New York before and certainly never imagined that a whole city could turn into one big drinking party. These two guys led us through the crowds from one bar to another, where we had to scream at each other to communicate or make frantic hand signals. That seemed like fun for a while, but then my voice got so scratchy, I couldn't scream anymore.

We were in a bar called Dolan's, a big cozy room with Celtic music coming through the speakers and lots of dark wood and pictures of old-time football and baseball players and boxers on the walls. Of course, Dolan's was so packed with human bodies that just standing in one place was almost a sexual experience. Nobody'd said so, but it looked like Dolan's was where we were settling in for the evening. I'd lost track of the guys who'd brought us, but I could see Margaret across the way, and I thought I heard Nancy's high-pitched laugh over near the bar behind me. Going through the motions of talking with some guy in a suit, I was trying to figure out exactly how drunk I was, which was pretty difficult, since the world around me was drunk, too.

It went on that way. I was even having what I might have called fun, except that it was such a peculiar variety of fun, standing in a swarm of people, making noises now and then, nodding, smiling, sipping my drink, spacing out, and watching all these strangers in an absent-minded kind of way. I was, of course, occasionally having to fend off a guy's hand from my ass or dodge around a guy who wanted to brush his triceps against my boobs, but these maneuvers were more friendly than hostile. I shouted to the guy I was talking to at the moment to ask what time it was, and he shouted back, "What difference does it make?" I realized he was right; it didn't matter. So I raised my glass to him, and we toasted time thrown out the window. It was about then that I realized I wasn't seeing Margaret and I wasn't hearing Nancy. The guys who'd brought us to the place had long since disappeared; I couldn't even remember what they looked like.

I didn't panic; I figured Margaret or Nancy would turn up before too long. There were so many people around, the bar was such a cheerful place, I knew there wasn't anything to be frightened of. I had my little party purse right there with me with my make-up, my ID card, and a twenty-dollar bill in it. But something in the back of my brain clicked on and instructed me not to get any drunker than I was.

One part of my consciousness went on with the partying. Another part went off into a quiet room and started calculating. It was possible that Margaret and Nancy had gone in separate directions, each figuring that the other would stick with me. Or it could have been that they figured I could look after myself. And I could. I was twenty-one, I could drive and vote and get a job and stop going to church and hold my booze and get married and have sex and make babies and do anything else I felt like doing. What I couldn't do was remember the address of the apartment where we were staying. This was a troublesome piece of forgetting. Actually, I couldn't remember if I'd ever known the address — Nancy and Margaret knew it, so it wasn't necessary for me to know it. I was pretty sure I couldn't remember how to get back to that building, but if I had plenty of time to look for it in daylight, I thought I'd probably find it; I remembered what it looked like. It had to be within walking distance of Dolan's because we'd walked here, though we'd stopped at half a dozen bars along the way. What my brain was telling me was that I didn't want to be out on the street looking for that building in the early morning hours.

When I went to a phone booth to try to get a number and maybe an address for one of the guys in the apartment, I realized I wasn't certain of their last names. There was a Kevin and a Bernie. And I thought one of them might have been a Williams or a Wiggins. The New York Telephone Company can't do much for you if all you've got is a Kevin and a Bernie with one of them maybe being named Williams or Wiggins.

Guys had been buying me drinks all night; I kept letting that happen. And I kept circulating, because after I'd talked with one guy long enough, he'd start touching me, usually no more than a pat on the shoulder, a touch on the wrist, a light hand at the small of my back, but a signal for me to excuse myself and move on. I wasn't angry at being touched that way; only I didn't want to give anybody the idea I might sleep with him that night.

The crowd thinned out. I didn't know the time, but I figured it must be around two. One of the problems with the thinning-out was that the male-to-female ratio went up drastically. "The majority of the males who were left were what you'd have called shitfaces, A.B.C.," I told him. "In another hour there were half a dozen shitfaces slumped at the bar, I was the only female in the whole place, and there were no more than a couple of guys I felt safe talking to. One of them was the bartender."

"You trusted the bartender, U.?" A.B.C. asked. "Don't you know bartenders have been taking advantage of girls like you since bars were invented?"

"What can I say?" I told him. "The guy reminded me of my vacation Bible school teacher when I was six years old. I'd have bet fifty dollars he was a Lutheran."

A.B.C. harumphed. "Sure he was. If I'd have been there, I'd have bet you the fifty."

I grinned, told him he'd never know whether or not he'd have won, and went on with my story.

My bartender announced that it was closing time. The guy I'd been talking to asked if I needed a place to stay. When I shook my head, he grinned, told me it had been real, and left. Funny, because I thought he might try to persuade me; I'd even considered bargaining with him for a place on his sofa.

One by one, and none too steadily, the shitfaces made their way out. After the last one was gone, I was still sitting at the bar. The bartender was washing a load of glasses, and I remember thinking, So now it's down to me and him. It occurred to me that I'd put a fair portion of my fate in his hands. He looked up at me and lifted his eyebrows. "Well, now, little lady."

"Can I talk to you?" I asked.

"Sure you can. But let me lock this door so we don't get any more drunks wandering in." When he walked out from behind the bar to the main entrance and bolted it shut, I figured that either I was in for big trouble or I was okay. This was a barrel-chested guy, mid-thirties, with a ponytail and a handlebar mustache. He had on a yellow, button-down oxford shirt that somebody had ironed meticulously — a wife or a girlfriend, I figured. Walking back toward me, he fished a pack of cigarettes out of his shirt pocket, shook one out, and lit it as he sat down on the bar stool next to me. "So what's the story?" he asked.

"It's kind of crazy," I said.

"I thought it probably was, but if you're ready to tell it, I'm ready to listen."

He sat with his head propped on his hand, smoking and now and then asking me a question, like what the building looked like and what else I remembered about the street and how we'd got here. "So what are you going to do?" he finally asked.

"When it gets daylight, I'm going out there and look for the place," I told him.

He gazed at me steadily.

"I think I can find it," I said.

"How about some coffee?" he asked.

He fixed a pot, and while it was brewing I helped him put the chairs up on the tables. Then we sat down at the bar again, drinking his coffee and chatting. Gregory Bates was his name, and he had a way about him of just calmly being there, not making me feel like he was doing me a favor — which he most definitely was doing. He liked talking about how it was to work in that bar. Since I'd paid a lot of attention to how things had happened this evening at Dolan's, I was interested in how Gregory saw it all from behind the bar. And he was interested in nursing. He said he sometimes even thought about going to nursing school. At the time, I believed him; nowadays I think he was probably trying to make me feel at ease. At any rate, we were talking so intently, and we were in such a strange little unit of time, that we went off into our own world there for a while. When I happened to follow Gregory's eyes and glance behind me to the windows, I saw that it was broad daylight.

"Why didn't you tell me it was light outside?" I yelled. I was gleeful beyond what anybody could have understood. I'd made it through to the morning.

Gregory shrugged and grinned. "Want me to help you find this place you're staying?" he asked. And I took him up on the offer. He had an idea of the neighborhood this apartment building was in. It took some walking and doubling back a couple of times, but we went over one block, and down another, and there it was. Gregory said so long; he'd better be getting over to his place to catch up on his sleep. I kissed him on his handlebar mustache, thanked him, and watched him walk away. That was when I realized something about Gregory Bates as certainly as if he'd whispered it to me himself: nobody else had ironed that yellow shirt for him; he'd ironed it himself. I shook my head and wondered why in the world such a piece of knowledge would come to me. Then I went into the entry hall of the building and faced a bank of buttons for the doorbell-intercom system.

It was no problem finding Kevin Wilson on the little tag beside the button for Number 3F. I had my finger poised to push it when I reminded myself that it probably wasn't much past six in the morning. That's strange to me now when I think about it, but I decided not to bother Kevin and Bernie and

Nancy and Margaret so early in the day. I mean, given the fact that they'd abandoned me for the evening, I should have set off fireworks and sirens to wake them all up, but for some reason — maybe it was Gregory's influence — I had this sweetness in me. I thought to myself, I can let them sleep; they've been up partying. They're exhausted, and I'm safe now. There's no reason why I can't give them more time to sleep.

So I sat down on the floor of the front hall and let my head rest against the wall. Like a propped-up Raggedy Ann doll, I stretched my legs in front of me. And I went to sleep. It was not a cat nap. I went way down into sleep. I think I even did some quite vivid dreaming, though I wasn't able to remember any of it. What woke me was a guy in a suit standing over me, looking down with a smile, and saying, "Good morning, Sleeping Beauty. Happy Day-After-Saint-Patrick's-Day."

After that, the only thing that happened was that I rang the doorbell and got someone to buzz me in. They were all four a little pissed at me for waking them even at that time of day, a bit after seven. Nancy and Margaret hadn't been at all worried about me; it never occurred to them that I wouldn't remember where we were staying.

A.B.C. was disappointed that that was the end of my story. It wasn't, exactly, but I had trouble getting across to him what it was that had stuck with me from that evening and made me remember it. It was the crazy little bit of goodness that came into me in the front hall when I was standing there all by myself with my finger about to press the doorbell, when I knew I was safe, and when I decided not to disturb the sleepers. That was the closest I'll ever come to knowing what it feels like to be one of the really decent saints, like Saint Francis or Saint Teresa of Lisieux. It was the only time I've ever had that feeling. When the guy in the suit woke me up, the sweetness had all gone out of me; I felt cranky as an old guard dog. When I walked up to that third-floor apartment and discovered that my so-called friends were pissed at me for waking them up and hadn't been worried about me, I threw a tantrum that shut them all up for the rest of the morning. It was a tantrum that cooled off the friendship between me and Nancy and Margaret for the rest of the time I knew them.

From about 6:03 A.M. until 6:07 A.M. of March 18, 1966, I experienced deep goodness. It was over and done with so quickly, I probably wouldn't even have recognized it if I hadn't been raised in the church.

A.B.C. surprised me with his interest in my notion about being good. Actually, I was trying it out as I talked. I'd remembered that trip to New York for years, but I hadn't told anybody about it since the afternoon I got back to Charlottesville and gave Marcy a report of my adventures. Only my telling A.B.C. about my four minutes of goodness did it get to be such a big deal. And now he wanted to know if it had registered in me in any physiological way (it hadn't), or if I'd thought about it a lot over the years (I hadn't), or if . . .

"Allen, you're trying to make it something out of a book, and it wasn't like that. You could feel the same thing in the next five minutes, and you wouldn't think it was all that unusual . . ."

"So why are you telling me about it, U.?"

"We're killing time, aren't we?"

"I'm not the one who made such a big deal about it. You're the one who told this whole long story just to get to the part where you took a nap."

This is the way A.B.C. likes to talk to people. It wasn't really a way he and I had ever talked before, but I'd seen him carry out these little play-arguments with Jimmy and Marcy. I took it as a sign of his liking me and being interested in what I'd told him.

But quibbling is not my idea of fun, so I shut up and just sat across from him.

He shut up, too, which surprised me. A.B.C. is not one to let a conversational opportunity go by. He seemed to be giving a lot of thought to something, though.

"Speak up, Allen. What's on your mind?"

He cleared his throat but didn't meet my eyes. When he began talking, his voice was soft. I had to lean over the table to hear him.

"I had this one time," he murmured, "when I did something okay. I was just now trying to figure if it made me feel that thirty seconds of sainthood you're talking about. I don't think it did. Suellen was about five. It was a Saturday afternoon. Marcy'd gone shopping. I was lying on our bed upstairs, half-reading a magazine, half-watching some kind of game on the TV. Suellen comes in, very distraught. 'Daddy, what's sex?' she asks.

"Something tells me to turn off the TV, so I do. And because she's so agitated, I begin answering her right away — no big deal, what's sex, easy question — and in as calm and soothing a voice as I can get myself to use. 'Well, darling, it's when two people love each other, and they blah, blah, blah.' I don't know what's chewing on Suellen, but I know she's needing an answer. She's needing it bad.

"Of course this is not an easy question, no matter who's asking it. So while I'm talking, I'm wondering what in hell has brought her up here with this on her mind. But I'm also wondering exactly how to pitch what I'm saying. God knows, I'm no child psychologist. I'm even wishing I'd read up on how to tell your kids about sex. I'm talking, but I'm feeling at a complete loss. Ordinarily, of course, I'd say, 'Go ask your mother.'

"I want to be as straight with Suellen as I can, because my

guess is she needs what the politicians call 'hard information.' But I can also tell that she's in a vulnerable state. Whatever I tell her will probably register more intensely than usual. I don't want to ruin the rest of the kid's life by telling her stuff that's just too damn 'hard' for a five-year-old.

"All this while I'm talking, I've got stuff running through my brain. Like, for instance, I realize my shirt's off, and I wish it weren't. I've always been a little self-conscious about having my shirt off around anybody. It would look too weird, though, if I got up and put it on. I'm also rubbing Suellen's back with my hand, the way I do when I try to make her feel better. It's an old habit from when she was a baby and I could sometimes get her to stop crying if I rubbed her back up around her neck and shoulder blades. It feels strange to be rubbing Suellen's back with my shirt off while I'm trying to explain to her about sex. But I put that out of mind and keep talking. While I go on spinning out my answer, I'm also remembering that this morning in the kitchen Marcy and I had this funny conversation about people doing it in odd places. Something she'd read in the paper brought it up. And I remember that Suellen was eating her breakfast while we were talking. We were both aware of her, and I'm sure our conversation would have been rated PG. Meanwhile, of course, I'm going on with my answer. 'Blah, blah, human beings are lucky enough to have this intimate way to express blah, blah, blah —'

"'Yes, Daddy, but what is it really?' she interrupts me.

"'You mean how does it work?'

"'Yes.' Suellen's looking me straight in the face, and it just kills me, the pain I can see she's feeling from whatever she's got on her mind.

"I take a deep breath and tell her, 'The male puts his penis into the female's vagina.' There it is. Sounds silly as hell to say it like that. Either I've told her what she needs to know, or I've told her what will ruin her entire life from here on out. Maybe both. I can't tell from her face.

"I'm feeling like the vampire caught out in daylight as I watch Suellen turning it over in her mind. Funny thing — I'm pissed off at Marcy for not being here when her daughter needs her. And I know that's right out there at the edge of my idiocy, but what can I say? I felt what I felt.

"All of a sudden Suellen's face crumples up. 'Daddy, that's what Kevin just did to me.'

"'Kevin put his penis in your . . . ?'

"She's nodding. 'He did!'

"Kevin is the neighbors' son, the same age as Suellen. The two of them have been playing together since before either one of them could even walk. Now I can see Suellen, in this hor- rified state, studying my face. She thinks I'm going to punish her or scream at her. Or some other terrible thing is going to happen to her. But at least it's clear to me now what was troubling the poor kid. All of a sudden I feel so sorry for her; I have the good sense to sit up and pull her close and give her a hug, even though I wish I had my shirt on. It doesn't matter. That's actually what I tell her. 'It doesn't matter, darling.' She's really letting the crying go on. And that seems exactly what ought to happen right now. I hold her close and pat her back and get a combination of tears and snot on my bare shoulder.

"'It's nothing for you to worry about, Suellen,' I say. 'I don't think you and Kevin are far enough along for this to count as actual sex.' I'm hoping this is true, though I can't say I know anything about it. Can a girl actually lose her virginity at the age of five? Surely to God not! What I know for certain is that no matter what it counts as, Suellen shouldn't have to feel bad about it. 'How did it happen, darling?'

"She goes on to tell me. They were in the bathroom together, sort of fooling around. Kevin wanted to try something. Suellen said okay. A whole little parable played out right there in the Plimptons' bathroom. As best I can tell — and I don't press her for explicit details — there was genital-to-genital contact for probably less than ten seconds. Can a five-year-old boy have an erection? I don't know, but I'm figuring probably not. Was there penetration? Again, I'm figuring probably not, at least not penetration as it would be for adults. Not the real thing. Maybe I'm just insisting on taking a Walt Disney view of this whole experience. I even ask myself, Am I refusing to see the real horror here? But how can it be horror if it's just kids — little kids! — fooling around?

"As Suellen talks, she calms down. I relax and rub her back while she sits there sniffling and telling me the last odds and ends of the story. Finally I've asked all the questions I want to, and she's told me all she wants to. She's getting restless, a little bored. So I lay some concluding remarks on her. 'Just don't go into the bathroom with Kevin anymore, darling. Okay? Fooling around with him like that isn't something you want to do again. Now you'll be fine. Don't you worry.' I tell her maybe it would be better not to play with Kevin anymore today. Then I pat her on her back and let her go back downstairs to work on her coloring.

"As I lie there, I'm tempted to go find Kevin and shake him till his little bones rattle. I figure I'll have to have a word with David Plimpton about this. Suellen had to go through the misery of fessing up to me. Kevin needs a little parental talk, too.

"I hate to admit this to you, U., but I'm lying there feeling smug as hell. I'm figuring if Suellen had taken that little story to

Marcy, Marcy would have exploded. Marcy would have made a hell of a big deal out of it, and that's exactly what Suellen didn't need. I'm actually figuring, now that it's over, that the way I handled it was maybe my finest hour as a parent. I made the kid understand she hadn't done anything terrible.

"This is the thing about what you're calling 'deep goodness,' U. For me, it's willy-nilly, sometimes good, sometimes a jerk, but either way, it comes out less than terrific. In this case, I was good, or about as good as I get. What do I feel? No serenity at the center of the soul for me. Unlike you, I don't get a sweet nap in the hallway of the apartment building. I get half an hour of self-congratulation, followed by the rest of the afternoon losing brain cells watching the football game on TV."

"Are you asking me to feel sorry for you?" I say.

"Yeah." He's giving me that old A.B.C. grin. "What's the matter, U.? Don't tell me you're coming up short of compassion for your old pal A.B.C."

Hang out with A.B.C. long enough, you'll want to kill him. I don't give him the satisfaction of an answer. Nothing makes him quite as happy as having me irked at him, so I grin back. "I feel sorry for you, Allen," I say in my best fake-sweet voice. We sit there, smirking at each other. Then this terrible thing happens. I'm looking at his face, that old face I've known for I can't count how many years.

I want the man.

I don't have a good reason. If reason had anything to do with it, I'd already be in my room down the hall. I'd be on the phone talking with Jimmy. I get a guilty little mental snapshot of Jimmy at home, waiting for me to call, but I can't hold on to it. This thread of desire I'm feeling goes back to Ray Charles on the radio this morning — no, goes way on back years before then, maybe to the first time I ever danced with him and got an idea of how his body worked. I make myself stop staring at his face.

"Time to let this place get along without us, U." He stands up and stretches.

His stretching like that is the killer. My face has to be red. I keep it turned away so he won't notice. I've got nothing to say.

We're paid up and out of there so smoothly it's like we're on a fast train ride to whatever's coming next. We're pacing down the corridors toward our rooms, way on the other side of the motel.

I'd always wondered what it was with me and desire. I could go for months and not feel more than the occasional twinge. I could get to the point where I felt like maybe I was finally over all that. Or like maybe Jimmy and I had simply used up all the desire that was going to come to us, and neither of us much wanted to do it anymore, even though we both wished we still wanted to. Then all of a sudden, it would be there, real as weather. Mostly it was Jimmy I wanted, and mostly desire dropped in on me like that at a time when he and I could do something about it — if Jimmy was in the mood, too. I could usually get him in the mood if he wasn't there already. But sometimes it was somebody else, a doctor at the hospital. The ones I worked with and admired. Or even this one orderly, a very shy black guy who — what can I say? — just did it for me when it came to looks. Almost always it was somebody I knew pretty well.

I wondered if it happened to most women like that — random attacks. I was used to it. And used to hiding it, waiting it out until it was gone. After I married Jimmy, I never acted on it with somebody else. Once I let a doctor kiss me at a staff Christmas party and was so ashamed afterward that I even told

Jimmy about it to make sure I wouldn't go any further with that guy. But the thing is, when it came on me like that, I felt like a slave — to what, I didn't know; slave to the invisible master, I guess. I didn't know if I was a freak or if I was typical. Guys are supposed to be like that all the time, victims of their glands, wanting sex so bad, they can hardly keep their flies up, and so on. I think actually women are more driven.

I tried talking to Marcy about desire, but she didn't like the topic. Friend of mine that she was, there were barriers she'd had up all the years I'd known her. "If something happens, it happens," a married girlfriend of mine told me once when I asked if she really was going to have an affair with this totally inappropriate guy. "I'm not looking for trouble," she said, "but when trouble comes and knocks on my door, I can't say I'm not home." What did she mean by that? I asked, but she gave me a shrug and this bitter little smile. Now I knew. Walking with A.B.C. down that last corridor toward our rooms, I gave my head a shake. I felt like trouble was knocking at my door, and I was definitely at home.

"My place or yours?" he says when we arrive at the side-by-side doors. His physical presence is radiological. I'm not looking at him, but I'm registering the shape of his body shimmering right beside me.

"Not funny," I say, putting my key in the lock and pushing the door open. I'm hoping I can walk my way through this. I may want him so badly, I can't even talk, but that doesn't mean he has to know it. I can just do what I'd ordinarily do, and he won't know the difference.

"What's up, U.? Something happening here? Please clue in your old pal Allen."

He's standing right outside my door. I step inside and turn to him, but I can't raise my eyes. Close the door! my mind is shouting. Just close the door! But some other voice is quietly saying, You can't close the door in his face.

The instant hovers. Then he steps inside. I take a step back but am still facing him — a short dance. A.B.C. reaches back to the door behind him and pushes it slowly, watching me. Now I meet his eyes. He eases the door shut so that, even though I know it's coming, the click of the latch startles me.

The room isn't totally dark. Light seeps in around the window curtain at the opposite side of the room. I know I need to say something, need to make a little conversation to snap everything back to normal. But the words don't come. While I stand facing A.B.C., my eyes adjust to the dark; it becomes lighter and lighter shades of gray that let me gradually make out the details of his face. It's like standing in a black-and-white photograph while it's developing.

"We can turn on the light, U.," he murmurs.

"Turn it on then," I say.

"You turn it on."

Neither of us moves. We stand like that, face to face.

He raises an arm and extends it across the space between us and touches my forearm, just below the elbow. He lets his fingers stay there, on my skin, long enough for me to look down at them.

Then A.B.C. and I are into it, what was coming to us sure as the clock striking midnight. We're nearly lunging at each other's mouth. We're crude and awkward — I probably cut the inside of my lip, banging it against A.B.C.'s teeth. And he can't decide whether he wants to undress me or himself, so I don't know which way I'm supposed to go with this either. We make it to one of the beds, of course, mostly undressed.

The instant before he touched my arm, I wanted A.B.C. so much, I'd have paid him to take me. Now that we're into it, I want him less and less. At first I don't understand it; maybe it's too sudden. Dancing together, those few times back in college, is the closest we ever got in the thirty years we've been acquainted. Now we're nearly naked, and it's a shock. What I thought I would like I don't like. I don't like his thumbs so insistently brushing my nipples. I don't like how his neck smells up in that hollow just below his ear, the place I'd thought I would so dearly like to kiss. I don't like how he pushes his hips up between my thighs and keeps on pushing as if this were exactly what I should want him to do. I'm ashamed that my feelings are traitors like this. I'm trying to get myself to say something, because A.B.C. is a train going down a mountain. Desire has been building up in me, too, all this time, so my body is still moving with it, even though I feel it starting to pull back. But A.B.C. is —

This monstrous noise rips itself up out of my throat, but it sounds like it's coming out of A.B.C. It's as if, suspended over me, he's taken control of my voice. Then I understand. He shouted; I wailed: it was one sound. I also understand that I'm crying now. A.B.C. gets that, too. He freezes. He's locked into me.

"What's wrong, U.?"

I can't tell him.

"Did I hurt you?"

I can at least shake my head. But then I'm nodding. I don't know what I'm telling him. I pull away. For a moment I don't think he's going to let me; then he does. It hurts when he goes out of me. I turn my back to him and curl up; my shoulders are shaking. I want to be covered — being naked is what's hurting me now — but it's too crazy to try to get up and fix the bedclothes over me. A.B.C. curls himself around me and tries to comfort me with his body. I know he's trying to make me feel better, but I don't want him here with me. I shake my head. He must get it, because he moves away. In a second I feel a cover softly coming over me. He's taken the spread from the other bed and covered me with it.

That's when the phone rings.

It goes on ringing. I get myself to stop crying, but I don't move. A.B.C. doesn't, either. He sits behind me, on the bed beside the table. I don't see him, but I know he's staring at the ringing phone. We don't move until it stops on maybe the tenth or twelfth ring. When the room is silent at last, he says, "He's going to call back, U. You better get ready to talk to him."

I make myself sit up in the bed. I know I've got to think about what's going to happen, but my mind can't let go of what I've just done.

"You want the light on?" he asks.

I shake my head. Talking is completely out of the question. I pull the bedspread around me because I'm shivering.

Still naked, A.B.C. stands up and walks over to the window. First he peeks around the edge of the curtain. Then he opens it — and snaps us into another dimension. The room fills with a dark yellow light from outside. Huge flakes are still drifting down out there, between the window glass and the black sky. This is what I needed to see. I don't know how to explain it, but the falling snow is as calming to me as when I was kid sick in bed at night, and my mother would tiptoe into my room and brush her hand across my forehead. I sit there, watching the flakes sift down. A.B.C. watches, too.

When the phone rings again, I pick it up right away. "Hey, Jimmy," I say. "I thought that was you just now. I was getting out of the shower." My voice is fine. And because he doesn't question me, that business about the shower is the only lie I have to tell him. He only wants to chat. The girls are still over at the Crandalls' house. He's feeling lonely, at home by himself. Poor Jimmy, I'm so sentimental about him that I have lots more to say than I would ordinarily. I tell him about the snow and the food A.B.C. and I had for dinner. I can see Jimmy sitting in our den with a basketball game on the TV, the sound muted, and a bottle of beer on the table beside him. While he's talking with me and watching the game, he's pushing his fingers back through his hair.

I know him so well that right at that moment his smallest habits seem very dear to me. I want to tell him what happened to me and A.B.C. I want to tell him not so much because I feel guilty — though maybe that's what I do feel and don't realize it yet — but because Jimmy and Marcy are the only two people in the world who could help me figure out what to make of it.

Of course, they were the two I could never tell.

Jimmy would have advised me to keep the story to myself. "There are no bad stories," he once told me. "But you do have to be careful who you tell the ones that matter to you."

Jimmy told the girls and me so many stories about his sister, Edna, that she became a presence in our lives, especially while our girls were growing up. They used to question him and ask him to talk about her so much that she was like somebody we'd all known while she was alive — Edna, with her huge eyes and her pale bony face.

When it became clear what was wrong with Edna, the family let their doctor tell her everything, including that she was going to die. This doctor was a maverick back then in advocating that even little kids be told exactly what was happening to them. "Everybody needs to know the news," he said. "When the news is bad, the person needs it maybe even more than when it's good."

Jimmy said his sister took it in a funny way. Or maybe she

took it in the right way; he wasn't sure. Leukemia was a neutral thing to her, a new fact she had to get used to. If she was sad or scared, she never showed it. Not that she was cheerful. Jimmy said it was as if she'd taken on an assignment for school, something she had to get done and handed in. She wanted a timetable. The only thing she ever complained about was that they couldn't tell her exactly when she was going to die. She thought they should have it down to the hour. Even at the very end she was asking questions about that, about how much time she had left.

Edna became the family director. She especially liked parties, parties for kids her age, kids Jimmy's age, even parties for the grown-ups. She liked planning these parties and deciding things at them. "Now it's time to bob for apples," she'd say. Or, "Now I think we should all go into the living room for our dessert." Even when she couldn't really take part in games or eat very much, she liked to be there, liked making the decisions, liked seeing people do what she thought would make them happy.

The family got used to it. Mr. Rago checked with Edna every morning about what time she wanted him to be home from work. Mrs. Rago consulted with Edna about dinner menus for the week. Jimmy said it was weird, but he got so he'd ask his little sister if he could have a friend over from school. He said Edna was very serious about the job, and she wasn't bad at it. Mostly she kept track of who was doing what and when, and she worked out decent schedules for everybody. He said it kept the rest of them cheered up, even when she started going downhill the last time, and they all knew it was coming. As long as she could tell them something she wanted done, they felt they could face whatever came next. "Edna says she wants these flowers over on that table," Mrs. Rago would whisper from

Edna's bedside, and all three of them would be reaching for the vase.

We knew it was a sentimental story. It didn't matter. We didn't tell it to anybody outside our family, and Jimmy usually didn't bring it up on his own. But sometimes I knew he needed to tell some of it. Or one of the girls would need him to talk about Edna.

"Would Edna tell you what clothes to wear?" one of them would ask. He'd have to think about the question; sometimes we could see him remembering something that made him smile or made him sad. But he never turned us down. After a while he'd start talking. The best was when he remembered something he hasn't told us before. The girls and I could get pretty excited when Jimmy told us a new part of the Edna story. There was the famous haircut that he came up with, where Edna had this young man who came to her hospital room and did up her little tufts of white blond hair so that she looked strange and beautiful at the same time. I knew it was childish of me, but I loved that new Edna chapter as much as any birthday or Christmas present I ever got.

The story of Edna had been going on since right after Jimmy and I became so caught up in each other in Charlottesville. We were taking a slow walk on the lawn one sunny afternoon in April. Jimmy had his arm around my shoulder, and I had mine around his waist, because that's how we were with each other in those days. In this voice that was like a tune he wanted me to learn, he told me about his sister.

The thought occurred to me so suddenly that I had to interrupt him: "Have you ever told A.B.C. about Edna?"

Jimmy stopped walking and looked at me with the most horrified expression on his face. "You think I'd tell that guy that story?" he asked me. "Not in a million years."

What he said felt absolutely right to me. Now and then over the span of our lives together I had to ask him the same question. More than once I needed to hear the answer he always gave me.

"Have you told him yet?" I'd ask.

"Told who what?" Jimmy would ask, though he knew perfectly well what I meant.

"A.B.C.," I'd say. "About Edna."

"No way. He doesn't get that story."

Then it seemed we could go on from there.

5

Goodness

WHEN I WAS forty-one I had a fifteen-year-old lover who made me extremely happy. After some months, she took an interest in someone her own age. I'm well past sixty now. The loss keeps coming back to me. Almost every afternoon, I find myself standing at my office window, hands behind my back, gazing out over the lake, and so pierced by Marcy's absence that I envision myself bursting through the glass and sailing down into the traffic ten floors below.

Should I ever do such a thing, the sole person on the planet who would understand is Marcy Bunkleman. She no longer lives in this city, but of course her mother would tell her about it within a day or so. Some comfort comes to me from knowing that Marcy would be informed of my suicide. She would understand it, and she would be sympathetic. At fifteen, she felt things very deeply; she cannot have changed so much in that regard.

The person I miss was — technically, at least — a child, and that person no longer exists. I suppose it must be that way with any former relationship — the people haven't stayed the same — but when your former lover has actually grown into adulthood, the change is dramatic. I counsel myself that Marcy may as well be dead. Should I encounter her again (which is not out of the question, since I am still on friendly terms with her mother), she would only vaguely resemble the person with whom I spent those enchanted afternoons in bed.

A jury of my peers would sentence me to prison. The prosecuting attorney would argue, successfully, that I had seduced the child. Seduce, however, is not the accurate term. I invited Marcy to have "an adventure" with me; she accepted. She was a highly intelligent person in full possession of her mental and emotional faculties. She made a rational decision. One may find the contract odious, but it was a contract, nevertheless. It was made on a Saturday afternoon by her parents' swimming pool. My wife and her mother, who were close friends in those days, were sitting some distance away, chatting and tanning their legs. Her father, who is dead now, had made his usual excuse to remain indoors. Marcy and I sat side by side at the pool's edge, lazily splashing our feet in the water. Without thinking, I launched those words out into the sunlight: "Marcy, would you like to have an adventure with me?"

Ten seconds before I spoke, I had no notion I was about to utter words that would lead to Marcy and me regularly coupling. The adventure I had in mind was one of intimacy, but my idea was essentially quite boyish. I wanted to be alone with her and to have physical contact with her, but until then — until I spoke those words — I had not even dared a sexual fantasy about Marcy.

I was, however, under her spell. I had witnessed her growing up. I had known her as a little girl, playing with dolls and stuffed animals. Very early in her — what should I say? — evolution into humanness, I had come to know her. I've read the

Nabokov book, which was certainly of interest to me even if a little off-putting. I was relieved to see that my attraction to Marcy was unlike Humbert's to Lolita. That man was generally drawn to young girls. I was specifically drawn to Marcy Bunkleman. Other girls her age were of no interest to me. What little contact I had with them led me to consider them insipid.

Marcy, on the other hand, from infancy on, possessed a lively intelligence that increased in brilliance as she grew older. She was exceptionally alert, and what set her apart was her calm attentiveness. Whenever I walked into a room where she was, even before she could talk, her eyes focused on my face. She waited to see what I would do, what I would say. She watched me. It was eerie when she was very young, because I could tell in an instant when I had lost her attention. Once when I fatuously asked how she liked school, she simply turned her back on me and walked away. Her father shook his head. "She has high standards for conversation," he said.

In the early part of my career, I did a good deal of traveling in the Far East. The presents I brought Marcy from Japan and India and Thailand appealed to her. She especially liked me to tell her "stories" of my travels, stories with children in them, if possible. It started with my telling her about a Korean country boy, new to the city and lost on an elevator and trying each floor in the building until he came to the one where his parents stood waiting for him. I'd heard this anecdote from a man with whom I'd negotiated a number of transactions; he told it as a story from his own childhood. Ordinarily when I traveled, I didn't see many children, so for Marcy's sake I began asking the businessmen I met about theirs. I watched families in hotels and on the street. I tried to engage waitresses and cab drivers and hotel maids in conversation so that they would tell me about their children. I confess that after I learned something I knew Marcy would like to hear, I jotted it down to be sure I'd remember it for her.

What I sought was Marcy's face turned directly to me; Marcy's eyes slightly widened and moving to catch every nuance of my voice, my expression, and my gestures; Marcy's pupils dilated, as if she wished to take my story into her body. What I sought was Marcy listening to me — completely giving herself over — because there was such intensity in her attention. When it was a good story and I'd reached a certain point in it, I could feel the air crackling between us.

I can't deny that her beauty, when she matured, had an effect on me. Even when I was in my early forties, however, I'd had enough of feminine beauty. In her time, my mother was considered a great beauty. In high school and college I'd dated beautiful women. I'd married a beautiful woman (whose beauty I no longer noticed). I did business with beautiful women. And so on. I don't mean to sound jaded, but I wasn't vulnerable to that aspect of Marcy Bunkleman. She was blond and lithe and graceful — a strong athlete in her school. She had high cheekbones and full lips, and her nose took on a few freckles in the summer. If you'd done up her hair and given her a black cocktail dress with pearls and put her in high heels, you'd have had a stunning creature before your eyes. Later, I did, in fact, buy her the dress, the pearls, and the shoes, though when she tried them on, they seemed to embarrass her. And even in her plain navy blue bathing suit that afternoon by the pool, she was a girl who'd catch any man's eye. It wasn't only her appearance, however, that drew me to her. It was that inner intensity, that power of comprehending me. With her face turned toward me, I felt profoundly alert.

Recently, while watching an ice-skating competition on television, I saw the performance of a fourteen-year-old girl paired with a twenty-year-old man. The girl's body moved with poise and subtlety. When the performance was over and the pair sat waiting to receive their scores, the camera moved in for a close-up that revealed the girl to be fidgety and self-conscious. She didn't know what to do with her hands. Flitting across her face was one expression after another. Marcy had been far more re-fined than this child. Yet as I watched that young skater twitch-ing and grimacing and half-smiling under the scrutiny of the camera, I was granted a slight memory of how I'd felt — as a whiff of a certain fragrance can transport one back in time — around Marcy. I'd never had enough of her. In my basement recreation room, by myself, watching a costumed girl on a television screen, I felt my neck burning with shame. It came home to me, sharply, that I had no right even to the few months of her life that Marcy had given me. Propped up on pillows and gazing at that girl lying beside me, unclothed, in a room full of sunlight, I was committing an act of thievery.

I am, as I say, of an age to retire. It has been many years since I experienced a feeling that approached profound alertness. A certain objectivity sets in in one's sixties. Because time has revealed its shape, one is more and more inclined to look back on one's life. One's rise and fall are evident. When I lost Marcy, I began to undergo the disintegration of my spirit.

My wife, Suzanne, and I are soon to celebrate our thirty-ninth wedding anniversary. Many years ago we reached a tacit understanding not to have children. I've long supposed I would have been a good father; my wife, however, let me know that the thought of childbirth made her deeply fearful. As always, then, we will celebrate this September 30 by ourselves. Traditionally, we spend the evening at the Lakeside Inn near Fairport Harbor. We have a meal that is very much to our liking. Afterward, if the weather is kind, we stroll through the inn's beautifully land-scaped English garden and take our usual places on a bench that awaits us at a secluded spot above the lake. Here we have what we jokingly call "our annual conversation."

Like many married couples, Suzanne and I have fitted our lives together in such a way as to provide us with psychological comfort. Each of us speaks and acts so as not to disturb the other. Sometimes, at a party, I may see Suzanne conversing animatedly with one of our friends and am astonished at what a lively person she is. I suspect it is the same for her; I've noticed her looking at me during cocktail gatherings. At such moments, imagining how I must appear to her, I've been surprised by my gestures and speech. At home, however, our voices and our personalities are muted. So it isn't surprising that, once a year, when we're outdoors in the evening after an elegant meal, we find ourselves with significant matters to discuss. It was in this setting that we reached the decision to put Suzanne's mother in a nursing home. Another year we decided, at last, to move to a different section of Shaker Heights. And most recently we per-suaded ourselves to review and update our wills. Rigorous as these conversations are, they nevertheless make us feel better about ourselves and each other.

Suzanne's and my seventeenth year of marriage was the year of my involvement with Marcy Bunkleman. I made discreet arrangements for an apartment where Marcy and I could meet when she was out of school. On the afternoons I was with her, serenity and generosity came into my heart. It was as I imag-ined saints must feel — transported, radiant, empowered. I as-pired to serve Marcy with higher and higher levels of devotion. I even planned to take her with me to Hong Kong, where I thought we might be able to live together openly. It was a mad notion, of course, but just possible enough to entice my imagination. Over there I was well connected; in that economy my skills and my reputation were highly marketable. I could make an extravagant "gift" of that city to Marcy. I once spoke to her, casually, of the two of us moving to Hong Kong and was pleased at her response, a high-spirited laugh. She took me to be entertaining a pipe dream, but I saw how easily I could persuade her to consider the idea seriously. So much seemed possible to me during those hours.

When I was at home, however, I experienced a malaise. For that I blamed Suzanne. Often when I returned from an exhausting day at work I'd find her leafing through one of her books on painters, the living room unkempt, dinner uncooked.

Suzanne's mind is excellent; her taste is highly developed; she is articulate and personable. Not exactly beautiful now, she was thought to be so back in her days at Oberlin, and she has always been regarded as attractive. She is considerate. She has a kind heart. She has stimulating acquaintances of both sexes. Although I never lost sight of her positive qualities, I began that year to resent her so deeply that her presence often made me feel ready to fly into a rage.

Suzanne apparently noticed no change in me. I kept myself under control — for several reasons, not the least of which was a fear of arousing her suspicion. I also realized that she herself had not experienced a change in personality or habits. It was merely that I, with my mind and my heart full of Marcy, could not discipline my eyes from finding fault with Suzanne. Marcy's taut lankiness was a harsh criticism of Suzanne's sagging amplitude. Marcy's energy mocked Suzanne's lethargy. And so on. In spite of how unattractive she now appeared to me, I was bound by an ethical awareness. Suzanne had become who she was — a placid, overly refined, physically slack, middle-aged, childless woman — in large part, because she had married me. If I hadn't, in fact, made her into who she was, I had certainly given her license to be that person.

Such self-knowledge ought to have produced greater compassion in me. It had, however, the opposite effect. It deepened my resentment. I felt trapped, and I was prevented from protesting or complaining about it. I became more and more divided.

I am an instinctively practical man. My business associates credit me with having a superior understanding of international markets — as if I devote long hours to studying and analyzing the available data. I don't disabuse them, but the fact is that I let myself be guided by instinct. If I have a difficult decision to make, I sleep on it, and the next morning I know what to do. I recognize that there is an unconscious part of me that solves the problems I face. I suppose I should give myself credit, but in my year with Marcy Bunkleman, I learned to fear that part of myself.

On September 30 of that year, Suzanne and I drove out to the Lakeside Inn as usual. For the past week I had been in a dark mood when I was with my wife, but on this evening we were both in good spirits. During our drive, Suzanne related a telephone conversation she had recently had with Marcy's mother. Patricia Bunkleman had confided that she thought Marcy was working too hard in school; she had no social life, and the only thing she did besides study was stay after school for practice with the track team. "I told her that Marcy must be at the stage when there just aren't any interesting boys her own age," Suzanne said.

I glanced over at her, but she kept her face turned away, looking at something out the side window. Nevertheless, I couldn't avoid asking myself whether she was informing me that she knew what Marcy and I were up to. Was she telling me that she knew and wouldn't interfere? I tested that notion against my memory of Marcy's first visit to the Marsden Towers apartment. Marcy had inspected the bedrooms, the bath, and the kitchen; she had called out a list of what sorts of snacks and beverages I should stock in the refrigerator. Then she came over to the living room sofa, where I was waiting for her. Sitting down, she curled herself around to face me, laughed in the familiar way of our teasing, and asked if I wanted to make out. She intended to mock my nervous stiffness as well as my suit and tie, but that was the moment I discovered that I did indeed want to kiss her; that was exactly what I wanted. Remembering that first embrace and kiss with Marcy, I knew Suzanne was not offering her approval. She may have been warning me that I'd better not be up to anything with Marcy. But I decided she meant nothing; she was acknowledging that I had doted on Marcy for years and would be interested in news of the Bunkleman household.

As was our custom on our anniversary, we ate slowly, savoring and commenting on our food and wine, even though I was impatient to finish this part of the celebration. I wanted to move outside. Suzanne was attuned to my mood; she sensed my eagerness. All day the weather had been warm and clear. We knew the garden would be pleasant and fragrant. Indeed, it was so. There was no breeze that evening, which meant that the scents of the herbs and flowers hovered in the air as we strolled toward our bench. When Suzanne took my arm, I surprised myself by pressing my fingers over hers. Instead of sitting down immediately, I guided the two of us down the little path to a ledge above the cliffside that looked out over the lake. This, too, was a familiar spot to us. It wasn't much of a cliff, really, a drop of maybe thirty or forty feet down to a rocky little cove. But on that windless night, the expanse of water below had settled into a smooth glassiness that brightly reflected the moon. Immense space seemed to open all around us; this larger dimension of the natural world was revealed to us without any of the usual haze or mist.

When Suzanne turned to me, I was in the throes of such excitement that I mistook it for desire. I locked my arms around her and began to nuzzle at her neck — in my love-making with Marcy, this was something that aroused her. When I did it — when I put my face right up against Suzanne's flesh — I experienced a brutal short-circuiting of my emotions. The woman I had wrapped my arms around instantly became repugnant.

I looked Suzanne straight in the face. "Robert," she managed to rasp out. "Don't."

Her two words showed me what I was up to, what I had apparently been up to for the entire evening. Jolted as I was by what I understood, I was nearly out of control. We stood directly beside a knee-high stone wall at the edge of the cliff — what was probably the only cliff in the whole state of Ohio high enough to kill a person who fell over it. My arms were gripping Suzanne. At the moment, so much adrenaline had poured into my bloodstream that I could easily have picked up my wife and flung her over the edge. So the part of myself that had brought such success in my career had rather neatly solved the problem of what to do about the aging woman who stood between me and my young lover. I held Suzanne so tightly that she could barely breathe. "Don't," she struggled to say again.

God forgive me, I nearly did it.

I would like to say that some better part of me won out over the hateful schemer who had planned to dispatch Suzanne. Under the immediate circumstances, I believed I was being merciful. I realize now that the schemer was still at work.

On two consecutive afternoons, Marcy had mentioned the

name of a boy at school. Her conversation had been so casual that I'd taken little notice of what she was saying. But my intuition had been alert. I began to discern that she was taking an interest in someone else, the boy whose name she'd been saying aloud. If I spared Suzanne's life, it was to avoid being alone in the heartbreak that was about to come to me.

I released Suzanne and began to apologize. "I had this sudden image of the two of us plunging over that cliff. That's why I caught you up like that. I hope I didn't hurt you. Let's go sit down. I'm dizzy." And with elaborate care, I led her back up the path. "I may have had a little too much of that wine," I said, as we took our places on the bench.

Once more I looked directly at her. Across her nose and cheekbones was a glistening of perspiration. Feeling the evening's cool air on my face, I knew I must have been sweating, too. Suzanne's eyeliner, eye shadow, and lipstick were in need of repair; her hair needed brushing. She was scrutinizing me with equal care.

"Golly," I said, shaking my head. "Wasn't that something?"

Suzanne took a deep breath, as if she were weighing what to say. Finally she spoke. "Yes, it was. It certainly was." Her voice found its natural register. "What got into you?"

"I think it was the port." I used my droll tone — the one she would recognize as my effort to be witty.

We laughed. And we went back to our old selves. My wife and I sat on the bench in the moonlight, talking about one thing and another for quite some time, before we rose and walked slowly back to the inn and to our suite upstairs. As was our custom on our anniversary night, we made love, but what was out of the ordinary was the way Suzanne studied my face as I moved toward release — just as she had on the bench.

A dark thing, though, had come to us in our moment by the

cliff, and it stayed with us in our love-making. It has remained with us to this very day. How to say what it was, what it is? Something like a spirit or a ghost? Perhaps an invisible and malicious child? It is not an entirely unpleasant companion. I relished its presence during the month that followed, when it became obvious that Marcy no longer enjoyed my company and that I had to release her from our intimacy.

Sitting silently on the bench with each other that evening, Suzanne and I realized that we would spend the rest of our lives together knowing that I had nearly murdered her. She contracted to go on. I contracted to go on. That much I understood at the time. What I have come to understand over the years is that the terms were equal. If I had it in me to murder Suzanne, well, so be it. She had it in her to murder me, too — or so I have come to believe.

It was never conveyed openly. Our invisible little companion has helped me to achieve the understanding. My first suspicion came one evening while I was washing the dishes and something prompted me to glance at Suzanne, drying the carving knife. Her hand seemed to clasp the handle in an odd way. Our eyes locked, and Suzanne's mouth took on the slyest grin, as if I'd caught her in an act of mischief. She set the knife in its rack with a flourish. "There," she said, "all clean and dry." I heard the music of her voice informing me that she didn't care what I thought of her behavior. Also, I've recently become aware that late at night, when I'm almost asleep and she comes in to change into her nightgown in the dark, Suzanne often stands beside our bed, hovering over me for some moments.

As I say, by one's seventh decade, one has acquired a certain objectivity. In my office, in the late afternoon, I stand at the window, gazing down at the traffic and receiving into my heart these less-than-beloved insights. More and more often in the twilight hours, I wish I could turn off the machinery. Nothing bloody or dramatic. Just switch off the old self like the car or the air conditioner or the television.

The question that comes to me in these dimming hours is whether a person can trust another person. Where is there any evidence of human goodness? One of my first answers is that goodness is elsewhere, because it is certainly not in me. Only the most deluded religious idiot would claim to possess it. And if it's not in me, then is it in other human creatures? Mother Teresa? Billy Graham? The tall Haitian lady who cleans my office and whispers, "God bless you, sir," when I leave the building each evening? It is very hard for me to believe that anywhere in the entire range of human activity are there acts of disinterested goodness. As I suspect myself — the man who chose not to murder his wife — so do I suspect my brother and sister creatures — my gracefully aging wife, for instance, who has become so attentive to her domestic duties and who even now is preparing a dinner for me that may or may not contain a dose of poison.

It's all right for us to understand that either we kill each other or we don't — just as we either have sex with each other or we don't. The reasons for committing or not committing the unacceptable act have little to do with love or decency. I accept that. It helps me to appreciate the blood coursing through my veins. Over the years, however, seeing things as I do has worn me down. My weariness relentlessly drives me back to the question. If goodness is not where one usually thinks it is, where is it to be found?

It has been my privilege, or my punishment, to live among well-to-do people. Self-interest and deviousness are so starkly evident among my kind that it's a miracle we can stand to be around one another. At our social gatherings I half expect us to turn on a weaker one — say, some bejeweled fleshy old dowager who's abused her power and demanded flattery for years but who is now failing. In someone's living room one evening, we'll simply rip this woman's body into bloody pieces. Savagery like that would make more sense to me than what actually does happen: we tolerate grossly hypocritical and harmful behavior — not to mention the atrocities of our stupid, simpering conversations — for hour after hour, day after day, year after year.

When the cars below my office window switch from parking lights to headlights, I know I've reached the hour of *l'addition, s'il vous plaît.* I must reckon with the bill. If things are as bad as I tell myself they are, why shouldn't I take a running start at the window and give myself over to the flying glass and the noxious air above Saint Clair Avenue? If they're not so bad, then I may as well prepare the crisp five-dollar bill I have ready to hand the cleaning lady, get my coat and hat, and head for the elevator.

So what's it going to be tonight, Robert?

My answer is the usual one. Home. I'm going home. I'm going home to my wife.

As to the question of goodness — it isn't anywhere around this office, and it won't be waiting for me at my house — though an excellent meal will likely be set on the table before me. But I'll tell you where it was once. It was in the curious heart of a fifteen-year-old girl on a sunny day beside her parents' swimming pool, when she looked across her shoulder at me, wrinkled her nose, squinted her eyes, and said, "Yes." It was right there, about half a hand's length away from me. Goodness was there — and I was clasping after it — when Marcy Bunkleman looked straight at me and said, "Yes, Robert, I'd like that very much."

6

The Lesson

I'M NOT the genius I thought I was in high school. And my first week of baseball practice down in Charlottesville taught me that, by college standards, I was just an average athlete. It took me about half a semester to see that my glorious future wasn't going to be handed to me along with my diploma from U.Va. High-achievers like me were all over the place — second team all-Americans, valedictorians, salutatorians, National Merit Finalists, and so on — every one of us coming out of high school expecting to dazzle our university professors and classmates but finding out that maybe, with luck, we could get B+'s and A—'s if we put forth maximum effort and did some effective brown-nosing. At nineteen, I wasn't prepared for the news that in the herd of life I was trotting along in the middle of the pack.

What saved me was having Jimmy Rago on my hall. Rago was your classic U.Va. take-me-to-the-party frat-boy. *Try not to flunk out of school this semester* — that was Rago's motto. Everybody loved Rago. And here's the thing: *this* guy was impressed with me. Out of the corner of his eye, he studied me. He listened when I'd go off on one of my opinion riffs. He picked up things I said, and he made his pals pay attention, too. Rago was one of those guys who need to have a colorful figure in their life. So he became my audience. Almost from the moment we met, I started performing for him. And on our floor, he elevated me into this legendary figure. I didn't know it at the time, but now I think maybe his building me up is what got me through U.Va. The rest of Mr. Jefferson's university may have thought I was nothing special, but at least the guys on first floor Emmett House considered me remarkable.

It's no accident that Rago ended up marrying Uta Schild-haus, my wife's best friend. It's no accident that the four of us ended up getting jobs in the D.C. area and buying houses ten minutes away from each other's out here in McLean. I'll be frank about this: Rago needed me, and I needed him. We're not stupid men. Both of us would admit we had this macho-symbi-otic relationship that was probably very unhealthy. The shrinks would disapprove, but so what?

Rago got what he wanted, which was to stay at home all day, diddle around with a few magazine articles, and spend most of his time doing the housework. That's what the guy likes. I don't think any less of him for it. And it turns out that I've got a talent for influencing a few congressmen to vote in ways that benefit my company's clients. Those performance skills I developed on the first floor of Emmett House turned out to be highly mar-ketable. *Step forward with aplomb* — that's my motto. *Act like you have charisma, and maybe you really will have it* — that's another. You shake hands; you look the person straight in the eye; you speak with conviction; and you deliver the spiel, two parts humor, two parts flattery, and one part information.

I did my share of bragging around Rago. It's what he ex-pected. He had to keep seeing me as his amazing pal. Rago is probably the world's most accomplished house-husband, but it embarrasses him. It shouldn't. Uta makes plenty of money —

she's a supernurse for the whole area of northern Virginia — and they live well. That's what I used to tell him. "Look at how you live. How can you be ashamed of that?"

After Suellen was born, I asked Marcy to give up her full-time job; the hours were too crazy. For a year or two, she did on-call duty at a couple of hospitals in the area, but then I asked her to let that go, too. She didn't exactly see it the way I did, but it was ridiculous for her to be working when I was making the kind of money I made. I have to say, I was a pretty smug guy for a lot of years. Every now and then I even believed that what I was doing was a decent thing to do.

The basic difference between Jimmy Rago and me is that he's not a disciplined person and I am. Appetite, whim, the mood he's in, the weather — all that determines how Rago's going to spend his time. At U.Va., the guy was shameless about sleeping through classes, partying when he should have been studying, and taking any opportunity to try to get laid. I couldn't live like that. Habits have always made sense to me. I find it rewarding to get up at the same time every day, shower, shave, put on clean clothes, eat the right breakfast, and get to work. Stick to a schedule, exercise, eat moderately, don't drink too much, get enough sleep — I don't have any abstract belief in those things; they just *work* for me.

My interest in girls didn't kick in quite as soon as it did with other boys my age. As a result, when I was about thirteen, my view of puberty was like a sober guy watching a party where everybody else gets schnockered. Not only did I see what fools guys made of themselves over girls; I was also put off by the whole sexual scene. All that touching and licking and rubbing seemed to me like a bad science fiction movie. Of course, eventually I did get interested in girls, about a year behind schedule, but by then I'd developed enough common sense to be restrained about it, to exercise a little discipline in that area of my life. Marcy's the first girl I dated, and pretty early on, I knew I wanted to marry her. In our whole high school, she was the only girl I truly admired. To be honest, it hasn't been easy for me to find admirable people in general and admirable women in particular.

I confess, though, that I always had an interest in Uta. I took a lot of trouble not to show it. The whole time we were in high school, I had no idea what was going on with that girl. It intrigued me, how she looked so amused about everything, but she hardly had a word to say. At U.Va., though, she and I took to dancing at frat parties. It started with me politely asking my girlfriend's girlfriend to dance. Then this energy just evolved. The two of us hit it off on the dance floor, and the sexual content of our moves with each other got to be pretty high. We made it up as we went along, and that dancing wasn't like anything else in my life. It was wild. Uta and I would stumble off the floor, both of us red in the face, sweating, fanning ourselves, and I'd think, uh-oh, what have I done? What happened to restraint? Uta must have worried, too, because Marcy and Jimmy made it perfectly clear that Uta and I had embarrassed them. They'd be cool toward us to let us know. But come another weekend party, and there we'd be, out there dancing and doing it all over again.

Off the dance floor, we had no problem behaving appropriately with each other. Fact is, Uta didn't have a lot of use for me anywhere except the dance floor, and I knew that. She thought I was a windbag; she thought I was a phony; she thought I wasn't good enough for Marcy — I knew, because Rago didn't hesitate to share such confidences with me. I didn't mind. Deep down, I thought Uta was the only person who really had me pegged. Everybody else, Marcy included, bought into my routines. The

A.B.C. show worked for everybody but Uta. I admired her for that.

No doubt, my admiration was heavily tinged by lust. But since I had no respect for such feelings, I was able to push them to the back of my mind. I liked to think that's what Uta was doing, too. When the four of us were together, I liked it that she kept quiet most of the time, all the while listening to what I was saying and making her judgments about me. When she did glance at me, it was with a cold eye and never for more than a second or two. So keeping my distance from her was not a problem. The truth is, I wanted Uta sexually a lot more than I wanted Marcy. But that was something I didn't acknowledge until several years after Marcy and I were married.

I don't think people these days marry the way we did back then. Neither Marcy nor I had had any sexual experience. In her case, she wasn't physically a virgin, but that was because she was such a runner on our high school track team. I was astonished to learn that that's what can happen to a girl who exerts herself at an extreme level — she can literally lose her virginity by running the hundred-yard dash. I think I'd even heard of that phenomenon before Marcy explained that it had happened to her. And anyway, I was grateful not to have to deal with a medical consideration on the first night of our honeymoon. Still, I have to say that sex, first night and beyond, was a disappointment for both of us. Over time, it got better — and I know that we both enjoyed talking in bed — but the actual sex never got great. Maybe it never even got good. Marcy was shy, and I was, too. In the privacy of my thoughts, I reminded myself more than once that sex was not my reason for marrying Marcy and that I was a lucky man to have married the woman I admired more than any other person I knew. She and I were fine with each other, especially after Suellen and Erin came along.

We were, for a long time, exactly what I wanted us to be, a husband and wife who had things to say to each other and who enjoyed each other's company.

You take the tiniest speck of suspicion or doubt about another person, and usually it just goes away. You don't see the person often enough to keep on thinking about it. Or the person doesn't matter enough to make it stick in your mind. But if that speck sifts down into a marriage, where you see somebody day in and day out and where your daily life is wired to that person — well, in that case, a little doubt can come to matter.

Maybe half a dozen years ago, I started noticing something that didn't seem all that odd but that piqued my curiosity. I couldn't reach Marcy at home between noon and two o'clock. Either the phone was busy or she didn't answer. I'd gotten in the habit of calling to see what errands she wanted me to run on my way home from work — and our unspoken understanding was that I'd call late in the afternoon, just before I left the office. But a couple of times, when I knew I had meetings later in the day, I dialed the house in the early afternoon and got a busy signal or no answer.

It wasn't a big deal. I remember asking her who she was talking to — and she said her mother. Or I asked where she'd been when she didn't answer the phone, and she said she was probably out working in the garden. I wasn't paying it a lot of attention; it developed gradually. Sort of without meaning to, I started keeping track of when the phone was busy and when there was no answer — and it seemed to be consistently that two-hour span in the middle of the day.

So, okay, it's taken maybe a year and a half for this information to make its way into my mind and get my attention. Still, what are you going to do? Husbands and wives have to give each other some slack. Marcy and I never read each other's

mail, never snooped in each other's checkbooks or eaves-
dropped on each other's phone conversations or tried to keep
strict tabs on each other's whereabouts.

I did *not* think she was having an affair. I might have been
less curious about what she was up to if I'd thought that was it.

Marcy's level of attention is so concentrated that when she's
with you, she gives you this sense of delivering her whole self
over to you. I mean, when you have a real conversation with
Marcy, she is just so *there,* so absolutely present, that she's scary.
That's a quality of hers — an admirable quality. But there's a flip
side. And you have to know her a long time — maybe you even
have to be married to her — to be aware of it.

Within herself, Marcy guards a certain territory. I don't know
any other way to put it. I'm not even sure she's aware of it. I *am*
sure that her skills in this regard are highly developed and very
subtle. She and I had been married for several years before I
became fully conscious of it, before I could begin to wonder,
What's that thing in there she's protecting?

I never did get the answer. I did, however, discover a couple
of things about my wife that were — how should I put it? —
noteworthy.

There's a little patch of woods that runs behind the houses
on our street. One afternoon, when Marcy had talked me into
doing some yard work, I discovered the neighborhood kids had
made paths all through that wooded section. I also discovered
the community college has a building on the other side of that
area — it's at the very end of Cole Terrace — and has a parking
lot back there. From my back yard to the parking lot was maybe
a five-minute walk through the woods. That's when it came to
me how I could get home in the middle of the day and observe
what was going on without much likelihood of being noticed.

Depending on the time of day, it can take me anywhere from

half an hour to an hour to drive from my house to my office. One morning I bought myself a take-out sandwich and drove back to our neighborhood during "the mysterious hours" when my wife couldn't be reached. I ate my sandwich in the car, in the parking lot. And then I took a stroll through the woods.

It's an odd activity, spying on your own home in the middle of the day. The girls were at school, of course. Marcy's car was in the driveway. The kitchen windows — and the guest-room windows upstairs — look right out toward the woods, so if Marcy was in either of those rooms, she'd be able to see me walking up through the back yard toward the house. In case she did see me and wanted to know what I was up to, I'd worked out a little story about having a problem at the office and needing to come home and sit out on the deck to think about it. I hoped it wouldn't come to that. I really didn't want her to know how disturbed I was by her mysterious absences.

It was sunny, a fall day, good football weather, a time of the year when I'm inclined to wax nostalgic about Marcy and me in Charlottesville, twenty years ago, walking over to Scott Stadium to watch the Cavaliers get beat by Maryland or Wake Forest. I tiptoed up onto our deck and sat myself down. The first thought that entered my mind while I was settling into my plastic deck chair was that Marcy's life while I'm at the office is none of my business. So what if I can't reach her during a couple of hours of the day? Her privacy suddenly appeared to me unassailable — in the exact moment I'd begun to violate it.

I might have persuaded myself to stand up and tiptoe right back through the woods and drive my car to the office — if I hadn't heard music.

A musical note or two is not a major event; I admit that. But the sound aroused my curiosity. I had no idea what sort of music Marcy listened to when I wasn't around. She and I liked things together — or at least I thought she liked some things I liked, Ray Charles, the Coasters, and the rock-and-roll tunes they used to play at fraternity parties back in Charlottesville. But what did Marcy listen to on her own? I didn't know.

So I sat still and listened.

Piano music. Classical. A record I wasn't aware we had in our collection.

It stopped. And I heard Marcy's muffled voice saying a word I couldn't quite make out. For a second I thought she might be having a conversation with somebody. Then the music started again.

I processed what she'd said; "Damn," it must have been. I processed it a little further and startled myself with the conclusion that Marcy must be down in the basement playing the kids' piano.

I knew she wasn't a musician. Marcy and I went to high school together. Not to mention having been married all those years. Wouldn't I have known if she was a musician? She wasn't.

But she was, because what I was hearing wasn't a beginner working on "Row Row Your Boat." It wasn't intermediate, either. It was Beethoven or Mozart or something like that, and whoever was playing it knew what she was doing.

It took some more tiptoeing around to the side of the house for me to peep through the basement window to the piano — and sure enough, I was right. I was so right that my face was maybe five feet away from Marcy's when I looked in at her. That face was hers — and was utterly different. *Radiant* is the word that comes to mind. She didn't see me because her eyes were riveted to the music book in front of her; I was the last thing on her mind. And I decided the reason for the difference in her expression was her concentration on the music. At any rate, she was my wife — but a transmogrified version of my wife. I flinched at the sight.

Well, I did go on standing there beside the basement window a moment or two more, listening to Marcy's playing. She may not have been Van Cliburn, but she was accomplished; I could tell that much from what I heard. She'd have had to be playing piano for a number of years to do it that well.

The first thought that came to me was that Marcy was planning to surprise me — and the girls, too; I was sure they didn't know what their mom could do with a piano.

My next thought, though, was that Marcy was doing no such thing. She didn't want me to know. It wasn't even a thought — it was a recognition of what that shining face of hers meant. She wasn't going to give that to me.

I was shaken, but I wasn't so shaken that I didn't take care about not being heard when I lightly stepped away from the window. Nor was I so upset that I didn't glance in the kitchen window before I made my departure through the back yard. Sure enough, the phone was off the hook. So that accounted for the days when the line was busy.

What about the days when there was no answer?

That was the question I couldn't let go of as I hustled out of my back yard and through the patch of suburban woods. I didn't want to think about it right then. Actually, I didn't want to think about it at all, but there it was, planted in my brain, already pestering me. I knew it wasn't going to go away in the days and weeks to come. This discovery about Marcy's music — harmless as it was — had made me ravenous to know what else she was keeping to herself.

Driving back to the office, I tried to lighten up by composing

an *Enquirer* headline: HUSBAND DISCOVERS WIFE'S SE-
CRET: SHE PLAYS PIANO! I tried to think of the entire episode in a humorous way. I even forced myself to laugh out loud
— and I sounded like a man forcing himself to laugh.

So I knew I wouldn't be able to let it go.

That was a Monday. On Tuesday, I drove back to the neighborhood but didn't leave the woods, because I knew she was
home; the car was in the driveway. I sat down and leaned
against a tree, and while I passed the time, I let myself hope that
there wasn't another shoe to drop. Maybe some days when she
practiced, she took the phone off the hook and some days she
didn't; she just didn't answer if it rang. I knew it wasn't likely,
but at least her car didn't leave the driveway that Tuesday. I took
that as a good sign.

Wednesday, however, I'd hardly settled into my watching
place in the woods when I saw Marcy step briskly out to the car
and back out of the driveway. And then I felt foolish, because
I'd developed no plan for what to do in this situation. Okay, so
I knew Marcy sometimes left the house during her mysterious
hours. Now I had to take on the more difficult project of
following her. I didn't think a great deal about her destination
or what meaning it might have for our lives. I just knew I had to
find out what it was.

This shows how crazy I'd become. I rented a van from Rent-
a-Wreck, and, of course, went the whole way with the disguise;
at the hardware store I bought striped coveralls and a matching
cap. I packed up my box of tools from the garage and kept
everything ready in the van, along with my sunglasses. If nobody took a close look, I could pass for a workman.

The next Wednesday I pulled the van up half a block from
the house and had to wait no more than three or four minutes

before Marcy backed her car out of our driveway. I knew I was a fool to be doing what I was doing, but I admit that part of me loved doing it. I felt bold and resourceful.

Marcy wasn't hard to keep in sight, and it was maybe a fifteen-minute drive over to this old neighborhood of Alexandria, where she pulled into a long driveway. The house was up a notch or two from the homes of people she and I know, a grand old stone mansion on maybe a couple of acres of land that were in immaculate shape. I parked my van at the driveway entrance and watched Marcy enter through the front door, but I couldn't catch a glimpse of the person who let her in.

I sat for a while, getting my nerve up. Then I drove in, passed Marcy's car, and went around to the side of house, in front of what looked like the servants' entrance. If anybody stopped me, my plan was to ask if this was the deColignys' house and be very surprised to learn that it wasn't.

Nobody stopped me. I got out of the van, fetched my toolbox from the back, and stepped around to the back of the house. There was a patio and a swimming pool with a sizable box of pipes, control valves, gauges, and so on. When I raised the metal lid on that box I could stand behind it, as if I were carrying out some kind of regular maintenance on the pool, and see over the top, straight into the house through a wall of glass. Most of that side of the house was one large room, containing a black grand piano. And Marcy was walking in at the moment I took up my station. Her face was turned away from the window and toward the person following her into the room.

He was a tall man wearing a dark suit. My first thought was *Thank God, he's old.* But I had to give the man credit. Dressed as he was, with a white shirt that must have cost a hundred dollars and a tie that probably cost at least that much, he looked sharp. His hair was gray, but it was thick and brushed back dramatically, like an old-time stage actor, one of those guys who would play Mark Twain or King Lear.

I needn't have gone to the trouble of disguising myself. The two of them were so wrapped up in their conversation that I could have pressed my nose against the window, made faces, and waved my arms, and I wouldn't have gotten their attention. At first I didn't understand what Marcy was doing at this house, because I still had the unshakable notion that she wasn't having an affair. But I didn't have to wait long before it became evident what these two were up to.

A piano lesson. That's what it was. The man propped up some sheets of music, and Marcy took her seat on the bench, fussed with her sleeves and her dress, and finally leaned forward to study the pages. The man stood behind her, waiting, with his arms crossed and one hand beneath his chin. He was so tall that his towering over her like that, especially in his suit and white shirt, made Marcy look childlike. When she lifted her hands and began to play, though, each of them took on a different appearance. As Marcy played, her back straightened, and her chin lifted; her arms and wrists and hands became dynamic and forceful in their movements. And the tall man swayed from side to side and backward and forward; his movements were so stiff that he seemed reluctant to be moving but helpless to control himself.

Then this man — Marcy's teacher, I supposed — stepped forward and placed his hands on her shoulders to stop her. The sight jolted me; it was creepy to see a man put his hands on my wife that way. He leaned over to point to the sheet of music and then set his right hand on the keyboard, almost on top of Marcy's. Leaning over her, his left hand still on her shoulder and his mouth more or less at her ear, he could have been whispering things to her.

It upset me to see that, upset me so much that I got a quick flash of myself stepping up to the huge window and rapping on the glass to put a stop to what they were doing. I'm capable of being jealous; I know that. And probably capable of deceiving myself about my feelings. But I have to say that it felt like finding out your father never thought you'd amount to anything or your best friend hates you.

Though I've thought about it a lot, I can't say I've come up with any great wisdom about the meaning behind Marcy's taking lessons from that guy. Since then, I've seen a piece on him in the Sunday *Post*, so I know that at one time he was this hotshot concert performer who took himself off tour but still made recordings every now and then. He was somebody who didn't have to give piano lessons to make a living, and I never did find out how he and Marcy met or how they came to their arrangement. I guess the details don't matter. She went over there twice a week. As far as I know, she still does.

I stood behind the raised metal lid and watched them for quite a while, long enough to refine my understanding of Marcy's relationship with her teacher. After working on that piece of music for what seemed to me a long time — with him stopping her and pointing things out and putting his hands on the keyboard and then starting her over again — Marcy stood up and stretched.

As she did that, she looked through the glass toward the patio and the swimming pool — and right straight at me!

And this just goes to show you how spooky this whole episode was. I touched my cap with my finger. I'm not sure what I meant by that; maybe I was playing the role of the workman, the swimming-pool maintenance man. But I also wanted her to recognize me. Isn't that something? I wanted Marcy to step closer to the glass and squint out there and realize that it was me, old A.B.C., her husband of all those years, come to spy on her and find out her secret. I wanted her eyes to widen and her hand to come up to her mouth when she realized she'd been found out.

It didn't happen. She stood there and gave no sign she'd seen me; she could have been looking at a flat white wall.

It came to me then that this must be the real news I'd come out here to learn. It wasn't just that Marcy had this secret life — which was, I guess, news to me but news I could live with. What made it hurt was that this part of Marcy's life tossed me right out of the picture. I mean, there she was, looking directly at me, and she wasn't seeing me!

I'd been under the illusion that no matter what she did or where she was, Marcy always carried with her some awareness of me. And that would have made this business somehow okay. For instance, if she was having an affair with this old washed-up musician, but had been feeling guilty about it because of me, why then I could have found a way to live with that. At least I would have been there with her. I would have been present in her thoughts.

In this case, however, I was utterly absent.

When she moved back toward the piano, her teacher came up behind her and put his arms around her waist. What an old snake he was! But I'll say this for Marcy. She removed those arms like a coat she'd tried on and didn't like. She moved neatly away from the man and stepped back to the piano bench. Now she was the one with the finger on the page of music. She turned to ask him a question, but he was standing in the middle of the room with his eyes closed, hurt because of the way she'd spurned him.

I confess I liked that part of what I witnessed the two of them playing out. I really liked it. If I'd suffered some disillusionment over being removed from Marcy's thoughts for a couple of hours a day, at least I had the comfort of knowing she had no use for this guy — no romantic use, that is. She was, in fact, using him as a teacher.

And that, too, was somewhat educational for me. My conclusion was that this old guy had a thing for Marcy, which was probably why he'd accepted her as his student in the first place. Marcy was entirely on to it. In fact, Marcy had to know that his romantic interest in her was what made him continue her piano lessons. So she had that quality in her, too — maybe a not entirely admirable one.

I probably know Marcy better than I know any other human being on the planet, including my daughters. I know important things about her. One is that, even though she married me and cared about me all those years, I never possessed anything she wanted as much as she wanted what that old man could give her. And she was willing to swindle out of him as much of his teaching as she could get. I wouldn't have thought that of Marcy Crandall, née Bunkleman, but there it was.

Off and on since that afternoon, I've worried about that little piece of knowledge — that Marcy would use sex, or whatever you want to call it, to get what she most deeply desired. It's funny, but I don't think she ever used that device against me — which is to say that I'm reasonably certain Marcy has been honorable in all her dealings with me.

The way I think about where I am in my life right now is "out here." By my own decision *I'm on my own,* as they say, and it feels sort of like floating around in outer space. Maybe I don't always know what direction I'm floating in, but I don't think I'm wrong to be out here. I think it has to be just this way. Maybe that's the news that Marcy delivered to me when she threw that blank look at me from where she stood in her teacher's studio.

Remorse is a useless emotion, as far as I'm concerned, so I don't spend a lot of time indulging in it. But I can tell you this. For all the things I've done in the past and for all the things I'm likely to do while I'm "out here" — a lot of crazy stuff, I confess — I've never been without my awareness of Marcy. That's still the case. I mean, who is it I can't stop talking about? The woman is standing right in the center of my mind! That's the hook.

The barb is that I know it's not the same for her. Marcy's free of me. She always was.

7

Girly-Man Recapitulates

THE SECOND TIME I called, she picked up. I put the TV on mute and said hello. "Hey, Jimmy," she said. "I thought that was you just now. I just got out of the shower." But she didn't sound right. Something was wrong; the tone of her voice was trying to tell me. I knew, but I didn't want to, so I took over the conversation. I tried to talk away what I didn't want to know. I told her I wanted to chat. And I started chatting — desperately.

I told Uta how the girls were still over at the Crandalls' house, but they weren't all that sick anymore. I told her what Katie said and what Jennifer said. I told her I was home by myself, watching basketball. I told her I was bored, and I missed her and I missed the girls, even though I'd seen them less than an hour ago. I was just blathering on, wanting her to interrupt me, wanting her to say, "Hey, Jimmy, everything's cool down here," wanting her to say, "Jimmy, nothing's happened between A.B.C. and me. It's okay. Don't worry. Nothing to worry about, Jimmy."

Uta didn't say what I needed her to say.

I'd never thought she would do it with A.B.C. Not because of me so much as because of Marcy. Uta and Marcy grew up together in Cleveland; they went to the same grade school. I never thought she could work it through in her mind, to do it in spite of Marcy. They were closer than most sisters.

Or else I knew it almost twenty years ago — that she and A.B.C. were bound, sometime, to do it. Whoever saw those two dance together at a fraternity party had to know the act was just waiting out there in the wings for them. Their bodies spoke to each other, and it wasn't a private conversation.

So I didn't blame Uta for doing what destiny had in mind; it's just that I'd admired her so much for not doing it all these years. While I sat there, I thought, Well, now at least I won't have to admire her for that anymore.

Hell of a thing to come down on a man when he's home by himself in a house he's used to having inhabited by at least one of the females of his family. A man may or may not be good company, but most women come by it naturally. Uta has never had much to say, but when she's anywhere in the house, I feel I'm with somebody. I can be in the same room with A.B.C., have him talk straight at me, and still feel lonely.

My father had this thing he would do when I was a kid. He started it after Edna died. For a while I didn't understand. Now I do. I'd wake up in the dark, and my dad would be in there with me — standing in my room, in the middle of the night. Actually, it wasn't long before daylight. He was naturally an early riser. Because I was startled, see, by somebody being in my room with me — even if I knew right away that it was my dad — I'd sit bolt upright in my bed, and I'd say, "What are you doing in here?" My voice would be touchy, because I was a kid and because he was my dad, and because I really didn't like it too much, his coming into my room like that. And he'd say, "I'm not bothering anything, Jimmy," in this soothing way, like I'd wrongly accused him. He'd go on, "I was just up, and I thought

I heard you moving around, and I thought since you were awake anyway, I might have a word with you . . ." The man would be standing there, hoping I'd wake up so that he could engage me in conversation. He had nothing special he wanted to talk about; he only wanted to talk with somebody. And I was vulnerable, because I hadn't gotten my defenses up, so after a while I'd kind of slide into conversation with him. My dad and I would discuss guys he worked with and kids I went to school with and what was going on in the neighborhood and his plans and my plans and so on. Almost always we got around to talking about Edna and how we missed her. A couple of times, talking about Edna, we both got weepy. Then it would be daylight outside, time for me to get up, and the day would start, and I wouldn't realize what my dad had been up to. In the course of the day I'd forget about it, even though he did it at least a couple of times a month for several years.

My dad was lonely. He'd get out of bed, take his shower, make his coffee, and find himself in a house full of sleeping people. So he'd wake me up and start a conversation. I was the logical one. He knew I wasn't finished grieving for Edna, either.

Poor old guy, if he were around now, I'd talk his ears off. He'd wish I'd shut up. I doubt I'd tell him about Uta and me. Or about Uta and me and A.B.C. and Marcy, because I guess that's what it really is. My dad would probably say the four of us ought to go on Geraldo. A group marriage is what we've got here, ladies and gentlemen. My dad would be amused. But I guess he'd be sad for me, too.

So anyway, back when this happened, I'd almost finished chatting myself out on the phone with Uta down in North Carolina in a Holiday Inn with A.B.C., when she interrupted me and said — in this voice from Mars — "I'll drop Allen off at their house, and then I'll come home. We should be there by two or three tomorrow. Will you be at the house, Jimmy?"

"Sure," I said. "Sure, I'll be here." I told her that the girls would probably be here, too, because they were really well enough to have been home now, except they wanted to stay over at the Crandalls' and enjoy being sick together a little longer. And so on and so forth. Because I couldn't imagine where she thought I'd be if not at home. It's not like I was ever anywhere else at that time of day, unless I was maybe grocery shopping or at the post office.

"Good, Jimmy." She had this poignancy in her voice, like she was calling from across a war zone. "I'd better go now. I'm very tired."

So that was that. A little phone conversation with my wife of nearly thirteen years, and my life had done a double half-gainer off the high board. Marital ker-splash was what I was feeling, as I sat beside the phone and stared at the basketball players on the muted TV.

Not that I was angry. Not that I was surprised. As I say, how could I not have known this was coming? And it's not that I wasn't willing to accept this as something Uta had chosen to do. Over the years I'd put her through eighteen varieties of hell with my own love antics. I mean, if Marcy would have had me, I'd have never married Uta in the first place. Uta knew that.

Also, I was a spiritual slut. That's something else Uta knew. I was missing what they call a center. *Do anything, think anything* — that was my motto in those days. Not that I chose it. It's just how I was, which didn't mean that I wasn't a decent dad to Katie and Jennifer and even — most of the time — a pretty good husband to Uta. But I was totally suggestible. That's what I was. Inclined to fall under the influence of any flaming asshole who came along. Such as — the number one example — A.B.C. That guy had just committed the primal act with my wife, and instead of planning a good slow method of killing the son of a bitch, here I was, saying, Well, it's okay with me, Uta, A.B.C., Marcy, whatever you want. How can I help?

Jesus, I made myself sick.

So I asked myself if this was how I'd always been. I didn't seem to remember much past being the boy with the really sick sister. That was when I was eight or nine. Then I was the guy whose sister died. Bullies didn't pick on me; teachers didn't call on me; girls looked at me with pained eyes. Could I really blame my spinelessness on Edna? It was a true thing that after she died, I had to seduce my classmates and teachers back into treating me like a normal kid. Was that when I learned to lie down and let people use me for their mud rug?

When Edna was sick, I took an interest in her and what she was going through. I became more and more attentive and helpful. I became more functional than my parents were, because they were distracted by what was coming — which they understood more than I did. Taking care of Edna became my job. When she got really sick — when she wasn't able to speak very much — I could catch her eye and know whether she wanted a sip of grapefruit juice or needed help changing her position in bed or wanted a back rub. It was all practical stuff, as far as I was concerned, whereas Edna's pain disabled my parents. Toward the end, they could hardly stand to see the huge-eyed bony pale creature their daughter had become.

After she died, I was lost for a while. Did I ever come out of that? My parents didn't, really. My dad was obsessed. He wanted to talk about her all the time. For years he was like that. My mom? Well, my mom got dreamy, like she was on drugs — which I guess she was for a while, drugs that made her vague and forgetful. And she stayed that way after she stopped taking the drugs. She wasn't herself anymore. That must have been how I came out of it. I started serving my parents — talking to my dad, helping my mom with the housework and the errands.

So maybe I did blame my pliable nature on Edna. I should say, on Edna's getting sick and dying. I'd become hooked on waiting on people, paying attention to what they wanted, what they needed. I was your number one house-husband. I took Uta her coffee and the paper in the morning. I got Katie and Jennifer off to school on time, saw that they had their lunch money and their books and their homework with them, picked them up after soccer and band practice. I car-pooled with the other moms.

"Girly-man" was what A.B.C. liked to call me sometimes. "James, my Girly-man, bring me a beer, will you?" And I'd say, "Fuck you, man!" But then I'd bring him a beer. A.B.C. had it just about right. That's what I was: A.B.C.'s number one Girly-man, Jimmy Rago.

It didn't matter, though, what I'd been or hadn't been, because that night, in the basement of my house by myself, when I finished speaking with Uta on the phone after she and A.B.C. had done their bad deed, I was nobody at all. I sat watching the Celtics silently struggling in the finals against the Lakers. Those athletes had their game to play, surrounded by thousands of people witnessing the astonishing powers of their bodies; I was alone, sitting in a dimly lit room, so weak in spirit, I might as well have stopped breathing.

Stand up, Jimmy. That was the first thing I told myself. I did it right away. I stood up, reached for the remote, clicked off the TV, and consigned Larry Bird and Magic Johnson back to the oblivion of the wires that had zapped them into my house in the first place. The house made little creaking noises of protest.

There was a wind outside; I noticed that as I stood waiting for my next command.

My wife was five feet eight inches tall. She kept her weight a secret from me, but she wasn't heavy. She had high cheekbones, green eyes, and shoulder-length dark hair that still had its natural color. She didn't have to spend a lot of time on her appearance. She could get into the shower and be looking good and ready to leave the house in half an hour, twenty minutes if she was running late.

Go to the kitchen, Jimmy. I didn't question the wisdom of this directive. Snapping lights off behind me, I moved my carcass up the steps and across the little hall at the back door and into the kitchen. I snapped on the overhead light. I switched on the other lights, too, the one over the stove and the fluorescent ones above the sink and the counter by the phone. I'd already cleaned up my dinner dishes and wiped down the counter. Nothing needed doing in here, so I stood in the middle of the floor and took inventory.

Alles in Ordnung, Uta would have said had she been standing with me. She knew it pleased me to hear her use phrases she'd learned from her grandparents. She isn't a talkative person, but there's a precision in the way she speaks that sounds almost like an accent. People who don't know her sometimes think she's a foreigner. For fun sometimes she puts a little Cherman accent into her speech. When she feels playful, she likes to call me Schatzie — "my little treasure." At such moments she seems to find it necessary to pinch my cheek. That part of her playfulness I don't especially like; it's as if she's teasing her nephew or something.

Call Marcy, Jimmy. I did. Again, I didn't question the directives that were coming to me. I stepped to the kitchen phone and dialed the number I ordinarily thought of as A.B.C.'s.

When Marcy answered, out of habit I almost asked to speak to him. Instead, I asked her how the girls were doing.

"You know how they're doing, Jimmy. How long has it been since you were over here? An hour and a half? They're just the same: talking, giggling, eating all the candy they can scrounge up from the far corners of the house, and watching television as if it'll tell them the secrets of life. You missing your girls?"

She was using her kitchen phone, too. From the noises I heard, I guessed she was crunching the phone to her ear with her shoulder and using her hands to put away dishes and pots and pans. I told her I was indeed missing my girls — and that was true. I was missing Katie and Jennifer, though that wasn't why I'd called. But of course I didn't know why I'd called; I was just following orders.

"It's really Uta you're missing, isn't it?" Marcy asked. "Your wife," she said in this flat way.

"I guess," I said. "It's funny," I said.

"I miss Allen, too." She was about to go on, but there came this slight catch in her voice. I waited. "But you know, Jimmy . . ."

I made a small noise to signal that I was still there; I was listening.

"I don't know," she said. "You know what I really miss? I miss how we were in the old days. Back in Charlottesville. Remember?"

I made my noise again. I wondered where she was going with this.

"That's really the Allen I miss. That arrogant, funny, flaming asshole of a guy. God, he thought he knew everything, didn't he? I haven't seen that guy for quite a number of years. I married him, and then he disappeared." When she laughed, there was more than a little bitterness to the sound.

I knew what she meant. I also knew better than to start bad-mouthing A.B.C. "I guess we were all different back then," I said.

"You aren't, Jimmy. Uta isn't. I don't think I am. What do you think happened to him, Jimmy? You're his best friend. You must know what made him the way he is now."

"What do you mean?"

"Sly. Always holding something back. You know that, Jimmy. He's a tricky guy, now. And he used to be so straightforward, he almost made us puke. Remember how he was about that stupid honor code at U.Va.? How he said he wouldn't hesitate to turn somebody in, even if it was his best friend? Remember how we used to try to shake him loose from that, and he wouldn't budge?"

"I think he said that just to get on my nerves, Marcy. He knew I told a lie now and then."

"Well, who didn't? Except Allen. I really don't think he did back then. But things have changed; I can tell you that."

I wondered if she'd called down there and talked to him. I wondered if he'd said anything to her to make her suspect the same thing I suspected. Something was on her mind. Something definitely had her riled up. It seemed dangerous to ask, but I asked anyway. "What got you going like this, Marcy?"

She didn't say anything. From the silence I could tell she wasn't putting dishes away anymore or puttering around. She was standing still in her kitchen, the same as I was.

"Did you talk to him on the phone, Marcy?"

"No, not since this afternoon."

"So what's up?"

She sighed. "I got a call from somebody I used to know when I was a kid. Back in Cleveland."

"And?"

"It was disturbing."

"Disturbing how?"

Marcy sighed again, except this time it was a sigh of impatience. "Jimmy, I don't know if I want to have this conversation with you. If Uta were around, I'd be having it with her. But I'm not used to talking to you. Doesn't it seem strange to you?"

"It's just a phone conversation. That's all it is, Marcy. I don't have anything better to do tonight, and you don't either."

Marcy was quiet. I could almost hear her brain ticking while she thought. "Okay," she finally said. "I got this call from a man I was close to when I was a teenager. I haven't seen him or spoken to him since I left home to go to nursing school."

"Close to?" I asked.

"Close," she said in this voice that warned me she wasn't about to explain herself.

"How'd he get your number?"

"My mom. He called my mom and asked for it."

"What'd he have to say?" I was still puzzling over what she meant by "close."

"It was weird, Jimmy. I don't know if I can put it into words, how weird it was. Part of it was how old he sounded. That gave me the creeps right away. You know how, even if you don't know them at all, you can tell pretty much the age of the person you're talking to on the other end of the line? Well, this person I used to know has gotten old."

"Maybe he thinks the same thing about you."

"Maybe so." Marcy gave a little nervous laugh. "Serves him right for calling me up like that."

"Why did it upset you so much, Marcy? Give me a try. I'm a terrific listener. Uta has me trained."

Marcy didn't seem to be listening to me, but she went on anyway. "He's a businessman. When I was a kid, he used to bring me exotic presents from India and other places he traveled. And he used to tell me stories about what he saw in these countries. They were great stories. I could listen to him for hours at a time. So I grew up thinking of him as a magical person. I mean, by the time I got to be twelve or thirteen I had a better perspective on him. Still, when he came to visit my parents — and he was very handsome and extremely well-dressed, and my mother just adored him — it was like in mythology, where Zeus drops in to have a few words with the mortals. The whole house just buzzed with the energy he brought in with him."

"So you got to be close to him."

"Yes. Close. I got to be close to him when I was — I don't know, just starting out in high school, I guess."

"And?"

"And then I guess after a while I started seeing him as a regular human being. I mean, I still respected him. But I didn't like being around him so much anymore."

"And?"

"Then Allen came along. I started noticing Allen at school, and he started noticing me. He called me up. Pretty much what you know. We started dating."

"I'm not following how this made your conversation with this person so upsetting."

"Well, for one thing, it made me understand the main reason I got interested in Allen. For me, in high school, there was everybody else, and then there was Allen. All of a sudden he was this extremely definite presence in my life. It was as if he had this energy, and most of it was focused right on me. It was exciting to be around him. I don't know how to tell you, Jimmy, except he was still that way when we were all down at the university together. Allen Ballston Crandall was obnoxious and bullheaded and stuck-up and insensitive and childish. And I wanted to be with him all the time. I felt that no matter what happened, he had the brains and the nerve to get us through it — both of us."

I didn't even want to be thinking about A.B.C., let alone talking about him. I had to change the subject right away. "So why'd this person call?" I asked.

Marcy didn't answer right away. I thought maybe she didn't hear me. "Your old pal — why'd he all of a sudden call you up, Marcy?"

I heard her take a deep breath, like she was trying to jump-start her voice. "I'm not sure," she blurted out. "He said he was still at his office even though everybody had gone home."

"Yes."

"He said he'd recently purchased a firearm. That's the kind of word he uses — 'firearm.' He said it was a very rare firearm, a work of art, a pistol small enough to hold in the palm of your hand, silver and handmade and engraved. He said there was only one of its kind anywhere in the world, and he said it came with only three rounds of ammunition. He described the bullets for me, polished silver, each about the size of a small capsule."

"You think he was threatening you, Marcy?"

"No."

"You're sure of that."

"Yes. I'm sure."

"So what else?"

"He wanted to know if I remembered the presents he'd brought me when I was a little girl. I did remember them, of course. I described my favorites to him — the Korean wedding doll that came in a glass case and the jade dragon with tiny ruby eyes that came from Thailand. I was happy to change the subject and get him to stop talking about the pistol."

"Maybe he was trying to have a normal conversation with you, and it just seemed strange to you."

"Maybe. I hope so. But then he asked if I could tell him what I'd thought of him back then. I did that — or I did it as politely as I could. I told him how impressed I'd been with his beautiful suits and white shirts and silk ties. I told him how I'd always liked it when he told me stories. Then he asked me if I'd loved him."

"If you'd loved him?"

"In this quavery old man's voice, he asked me, 'Marcy, in all those thousands of minutes we spent together, were any of them minutes in which you were aware of feeling love for me?'"

"Jesus, Marcy. What did you say?"

"I couldn't make myself say anything. Nothing came to me to be said, not a single word. The silence just stretched out."

"So what happened?"

"After it had gone on for maybe a full minute, he cleared his throat and said, 'All right, Marcy.' And hung up."

"That's creepy, all right. So what do you think? He called you up after all these years to ask you that question, right? And even though you didn't give him an answer, you gave him an answer, right?"

I knew I was blathering on way too much, but I also knew that I had to keep making noise for a while, because Marcy had talked her way into a bad place. I thought I could hear her crying at the other end of the line. I thought there were probably some things about this guy she wasn't telling me, but I knew better than to ask.

"You know, Marcy," I went on, "this guy probably just took a notion. He's in his office; it's late in the day; there isn't anybody around. He thought to himself, Why don't I call up my old friend Marcy and see how she's doing? I don't think he meant anything by what he was asking you. He probably wondered what you thought of him after all these years, and maybe he did hope you'd loved him. He wouldn't be the only one who did that. Remember that day I came over to your house and told you I loved you? You're just too much woman for us all, Marcy. Men fall for you left and right all the time. Must have been happening since you were a kid."

"You're a sweetheart, Jimmy. You really are."

My motto is, if you make enough noise, you can bring anybody around. They'll cheer up just to get you to shut up. "And anyway, it doesn't matter," I said. "Tomorrow afternoon our dear spouses will be back home, and our lives will pick right up and go on. Let that guy sink back into oblivion, where he belongs."

There was a pause. Then Marcy said, "Remember to tell Uta to call me when she has a chance." She sounded tired now, like she was about to fall asleep that very minute.

"Right. I'll tell her. And Marcy, you did the right thing. There wasn't any way you could answer that guy's question. Nobody has a right to call up and ask you something like that. Even if you could have given him an answer, you shouldn't have. Keeping quiet was just what you should have done."

"Thanks, Jimmy. I appreciate that. See you tomorrow. When you come to get your girls."

I didn't mind that she didn't say good-bye. What I minded was that I'd done it again, picked up on somebody else's needs and scrambled around trying to fill them. I mean, what the hell? Girly-man rescues Marcy Crandall. Meanwhile, what's happened to Girly-man? Does he have no needs of his own that are worth mentioning? Is the man not a man at all but only a figment of everybody's imagination?

These were not the ideal thoughts to entertain in the brightly lit kitchen of my empty house. I had this flash of empathy with Marcy's pal — an old guy alone in his office on a spring evening, remembering a young girl. When a man gets cornered by his own loneliness, he's likely to do something inappropriate. That was my insight of the moment.

I thought about Uta and A.B.C. It was an involuntary lurch of my brain, because I'd been shutting it out, what they might have been doing right then. However much my imagination might be informing me of what they'd done, I didn't have any desire to make up dirty pictures of them in their North Carolina Holiday Inn. But my brain went ahead anyway, conjured up a bed in that ugly gray light that always seeps into a motel room. I even saw a clock on the bedside table with red digits floating the time out into the dark — 11:03 there, the same as it was here.

Uta was in that bed by herself. Surprised as I was, I knew it as certainly as I knew what time it was. I saw her lying on her side, with one bare arm outside the cover. Her eyes were open. She wasn't sleeping. And the light over her was somehow horrible in my mind's eye, as if she were buried beneath the whole roomful of that grainy dimness. I tried to see how her face looked, but the features weren't clear to me. I couldn't even see her eyes, except for the tiniest glassy reflection now and then. I thought she probably wasn't crying, but I couldn't be sure. I recognized that even if it was just in my imagination, this was maybe the saddest I'd ever seen my wife.

My brain took me into the room next door, where A.B.C. was also in bed by himself, in the dark, lying on his back and staring up at the ceiling. His hands were behind his head, his elbows spread out like mutated wings. This was somebody I'd studied — whether I wanted to or not — for half my life. He, too, was buried in a roomful of grainy dimness, and my brain struggled to bring his face into focus. What I could see was that his jaw was set. His whole body was tense, even though he was supposedly trying to fall asleep. I recoiled from the sight. It was like watching somebody inflicting pain on himself.

My brain let me move back from seeing A.B.C. scheming through the night in his motel bed. I felt relief. For the past twenty-some years, I'd been giving more attention to A.B.C.'s life than to my own. I didn't have to do that anymore.

I was free.

Without meaning to, with what they'd done, Uta and A.B.C. had granted me my freedom.

As I came back to myself in the kitchen, my last flash of insight was that Marcy wasn't going to tell A.B.C. about the disturbing phone call she'd gotten. I don't know why I appreciated that news so much, but I did. I knew it didn't mean Marcy was bound to me in any particular way. But it did mean that I was better off than A.B.C. I was a hell of a lot better off.

I went to bed and, so far as I know, went straight to sleep.

Next morning, I still had the house to myself, but now, in the daylight, it seemed a luxury. I figured I'd go over to the Crandalls' to pick up the girls around ten-thirty or eleven. I spent a couple of hours puttering around, straightening up one room and then another, finding places that needed dusting or spot-vacuuming, rearranging knickknacks and books and magazines and houseplants. There were lots of times when I'd complained to Katie and Jennifer about leaving a trail of mess behind them wherever they walked through the house, and I'd complained to Uta that we lived like pigs and the house was nearly unlivable. But this morning, I lost myself in tidying up. I liked moving through the rooms, bringing about improvements. I felt lucky to have a house like this, full of rooms where a family could live and be comfortable.

As was the custom with the Crandalls and the Ragos, I walked in the back door to the Crandalls' house without knocking and found Marcy in the kitchen, where I expected her to be. Even as close as the two families were, Marcy and I didn't hug. Neither did A.B.C. and Uta — but for different reasons. In the past, Uta was always at least half mad at A.B.C. — which was pretty much how he liked her to be — whereas Marcy and I were overly aware of how sweet I'd been on her all those years. So that morning she and I didn't hug, even though the glad-to-see-you way she looked at me was nearly as good as a major embrace. "Just made some coffee, Jimmy," she said. "How about a cup?"

Of course I didn't refuse. I sat right down with her at her kitchen table. We didn't eat anything, but we had the coffee, which tasted good enough by itself. I liked it that Marcy didn't try to impress people. A few years ago she entered a phase of fashion austerity. Unless she was going out, she wore plain blouses tucked into khaki slacks and no make-up. Her hair was cut short. She looked as if she was trying to remove all the sex appeal from her appearance. To me, though, she still looked as pretty as the eighteen-year-old girl I first met in Charlottesville, half a lifetime ago. Her face just did it for me. Ordinarily, Marcy guarded her emotions the way most people do — and I didn't mind that; I liked her anyway — but this morning it was as if she'd removed the veil for me. What she felt was right there for me to read — in the tiny winces, frowns, tics, and mocking and smiling movements of her mouth and nose and the skin around her eyes. I could have entertained myself all day, watching her read the newspaper. I felt almost guilty for looking at her.

"I got some sleep last night after I talked with you," she said.

"That's good, Marcy. That's terrific."

Our conversation was remarkable only in how ordinary it was, but it meant something to me, being with her in the kitchen, with the coffee and the feeling of something being exchanged between us. Then it was time for me to take the girls home.

Katie and Jennifer and I made our way out the back door in a confusion of backpacks and pillows and stuffed animals. Suellen and Erin Crandall were screaming good-byes to the Rago girls, and Marcy and I were rolling our eyes and enjoying the obvious and incorrigible health of our kids. I got this urge to give Marcy a good-bye peck on the cheek, just a dry little kiss, but something told me no, told me a definite, unambiguous no. So I didn't. I lifted my hand to her; she lifted hers to me. And I had the whole sunny day before me, and my girls and my car and my house.

"Dad, will you tell us an Edna story?" Jennifer asked the minute I put the car in gear. Hearing my sister's name like that was a little bolt of sadness; it always happened when I hadn't thought about her for a while. It was months since anybody in the family had asked for an Edna story; I was caught off guard.

"Why is an Edna story so essential right now?" I asked. "What if I get arrested for not paying attention to the traffic because of telling you guys an Edna story?" This, too, was part of the ritual; I would resist telling the story until I was persuaded to do so.

"We were trying to make Suellen and Erin understand about

Edna," Katie said, leaning across into the front seat. "They don't believe us. They think you're making her up. You're not doing that, are you? We know you're not."

I was trying to adjust to the fact that my girls had told the Crandall kids about Edna. I didn't know why I'd always thought Edna was a subject we'd keep among ourselves — in the family. I couldn't be mad at the girls for telling, but I wished they hadn't. "No, I'm not making her up," I said in a sadder tone than I really meant to use.

I was troubled by what my girls were saying, but I was also thinking that maybe an Edna story was what all three of us needed. Even if she was dead, my sister still had the power to put us right with one another as well as with the world outside our family. "You have to ask me a question," I said — as I always did. "You know I can't just think of something unless you ask me a question."

There was a pause while Katie and Jennifer sat back in their seats and put their minds to deciding on the right question. Finally Katie, the older one, asked, "What about playing, Dad? How did Edna play when she was so sick?" And Jennifer chimed in, "Yeah, that's a good question. Like, did you get special toys for her?"

For a moment I made myself remember the way we used to play, and then I started talking. "For a while her regular toys worked just fine — especially dolls. You know me, the older brother. If my sister is okay, I ignore her dolls like they've got bad breath. But if she's sick, the way Edna was, well, then I take an interest in her dolls because I know it makes her feel better if I do. And card games. We played a lot of card games with her, but she got to be better at all of them than we were. She'd play with my dad and my mom and me — so she was playing three times more than each one of us was. She got to be a whiz at go fish and canasta and crazy eights. Later, though, it was too hard for her to hold on to the cards."

"That's what I mean, Dad. How could she play when she was really sick? She was still a kid. Didn't she need to play?"

"Yes, she was still a kid. And she didn't need to play as much as other kids her age. But she did still need to play, I think. We had this game that didn't require anything except saying a few words, mostly yes and no. It's where one person pretends to be somebody, and the other people have to ask questions and try to guess who the person is. You know, like you pretend to be a movie star or somebody in a book, and everybody has to ask you things like 'Are you male or female? Are you on TV? Are you famous?' until they guess who you are. Edna was good at that, too, if she wasn't too tired. My dad, though, made a joke out of it. Every time it was his turn to be somebody, he'd pick Lassie. We'd ask, 'Are you male or female?' and he'd say, 'Woof-woof.' Your grandmother and I would get furious at him, because it was so ridiculous, but he wouldn't give it up; he did the same thing every time we played. And Edna always was amused by him. It always made her smile. Even when your grandmother and I were rolling our eyes at each other and wanting to kick him, Edna would smile at him for saying 'Woof-woof.'"

There was an interval of silence, as there almost always was at the end of an Edna story. Then Jennifer said, "Woof-woof," and I said, "Exactly so. 'Woof-woof.' Just like that," and Katie woof-woofed, too, and then asked if we could play the game at home sometime. I said it was a good game to play on long car trips, when everybody got bored, so we agreed we'd save it for the summer, driving out to Cleveland to visit their grandmother.

When we got home, the weather was so warm and sunny, I was wishing they'd want to go for a walk or something out-doorsy. But the girls did what they wanted to do, which was fix themselves a snack and clatter down the steps to the TV room. They left me sitting in the living room, wondering why they hadn't pursued the question of whether the Edna stories were real or not. I was sure that the earliest Edna stories were real, but I had my doubts about the later ones. This most recent Edna story seemed to me pretty real — I could remember my father doing that Lassie routine at least a couple of times — but I also knew that I made up a lot of each story. I didn't do it on purpose. It was just the way the stories came out when I told them. I wondered if I ought to feel bad.

I was still daydreaming on the sofa, a magazine open on my lap, when I realized that Uta's car had turned onto our street. I'd developed peculiar skills because I was in the house all the time. So many days I'd been here, thinking of Uta driving home from work, that my ears automatically picked up the sound of her car when it turned the corner of our block.

I was suddenly anxious. I walked out onto the front porch and watched Uta's Volvo wagon glide, not into the driveway, but directly to the front of the house. At the open window of the passenger side, Uta's face was turned toward me on the porch. I'd never seen her in such a state. Though the car window was open and she was less than ten yards away, she said nothing; she just looked at me with her eyes wide and her mouth so tense that she seemed to be forcing herself to keep quiet.

Then A.B.C. stepped out of the driver's side. He looked ap-palling, but it wasn't pain or terror on his face. He was angry as hell. Apparently he'd skipped shaving and combing his hair this morning. His shirt was misbuttoned, so that one side of the collar was higher than the other. "Hello there, James!" he shouted from the street. "Come down here and greet your wife and your old pal!" He was shouting at me as if he were drunk, but I knew that couldn't be the case.

I put my hands in my pockets and walked down the steps, watching Uta as I approached the car. I did this even though I knew A.B.C. was coming around the car, as if he meant to assault me. I was aware of A.B.C.'s excellent physical condition and of my own fat feebleness. But it was Uta's face that commanded my attention. When I got closer, she mouthed something that I was pretty certain was "He's crazy."

"You know, James, while your wife and I were on the road today, I had some time to think about you." Even though he was close enough to me to whisper, he kept shouting, and I thought I'd better not provoke him. "You sit around the house all day and let your wife make a living for the family. But I'll bet the only thinking you ever do is when I come over here and challenge you. The only decent reading you ever do is when I bring a book over here and tell you to read it. Your conversation is boring, James. You don't have any opinions." He stepped forward and moved so close to me, I had to take a step back. "I think you're scared, James."

The whole time he was making this speech, A.B.C. was sticking his face right up into my face like a baseball manager arguing with an umpire. His head was poked forward and his jaw jutted out. I might have said something back to him, except that was the moment it occurred to me that whatever his problem was, it probably didn't have much to do with me.

He pushed forward again, so I had to lean back from him. "Your girls are going to grow up thinking the man of the house has got to be their mommy, because their dad is such a *sweetie*."

These words he yelled right in my face, a little spray of spit coming with them. With my hands still in my pockets, I kept staring at him.

When I didn't respond, he forced me back another step. "You know what your problem is, James?" Using two fingers, he tapped what he had to say right into my chest: "You don't have a *you* in there!"

He waited, his head poked forward, his face contorted, his breathing hoarse.

"Woof-woof, A.B.C.," I said in this very quiet voice. I knew immediately I'd done the right thing. "Woof-woof," I said again, as reasonably as if I were debating with Aristotle.

He gave me one furious look before turning to Uta in the car. And the look he gave her must have been something to see. At any rate, he turned like a toy soldier and started striding up the middle of the street. Our block is a quiet one, trees and shade and not much traffic. I was able to watch him make his way all the way to the end of the block.

Uta stepped out of the car and stood beside me, watching him go. "He woke me up at the crack of dawn and wouldn't let me pack or anything. He drove like a crazy man all the way here. It's a wonder he didn't have a wreck or get stopped by the cops," she said quietly.

I was glad to hear her talking. Her voice, after A.B.C.'s shouting, was consoling. In spite of everything I'd been through, I found myself grinning at her. The look she gave me was a long story with several varieties of pain and struggle in it. "Are you going to ask me what happened, Jimmy?" she whispered.

I thought about it. I could imagine A.B.C. standing out here on the street watching us, with his arms crossed and a smirk on his face. "Go ahead, Girly-man," he'd say. "Give her your answer."

"I don't think so, Uta," I said. "I think I can wait for that story." Her face told me she was grateful.

Then she and I started unpacking the station wagon. The whole rear compartment was a mess. She said she'd had to throw in what she could of her stuff, because A.B.C. had been screaming at her to hurry it up so they could get on the road. There were bags of our things and the Crandalls' gear that Marcy and I hadn't wanted to carry back on the plane. "What a bunch of CRAP!" Uta said, startling me with how irked she was. "Just the sight of it makes me want to turn around and walk away." Her face was red, she was exhausted, and now that it didn't matter anymore, she was ready to lose her composure.

"Come on, Uta," I said. "Grab a little something. We'll get it. We've got all day to unpack this thing. We'll get the girls out here to help us. We'll make a party of it!" I plucked out a beach umbrella with one hand and a wad of dirty clothes with the other. And then I performed my incompetent juggling routine, where I throw everything up in the air and let it fall around me. This time I was unusually successful. The umbrella clattered. Our dirty clothes bloomed in the air and spread onto the sidewalk and the street — underwear and T-shirts and socks. Uta may have been about to cry, but in spite of herself she was grinning at me and shaking her head. I knew what the moment called for, even if it meant I had to split my pants. I slid into the pose, kneeling, with my arms spread out and my teeth to the sky.

8

Summer Afternoon

LOUISE'S HAIR was copper-gold. When it caught the sunlight, with a breeze wafting it across her forehead, I wanted to fall down and prostrate myself in front of her. I wanted to do something about the sheer *sight* of her! She and I were thirteen. And at camp.

Robert is/was the opposite of Louise. Reason enough, I suppose, for me to marry him. Do you know the Wyeth painting *Wind from the Sea*? That's how I think of the Robert of those days. In most ways he was as oppressive as the thick, dark edges of the picture, but his intelligence was the block of light at the center, the opening, the steady, refreshing wind blowing the curtains inward. He was sickness and health, prison and freedom, all at once.

It was like waking up in the middle of a lake — that's how Louise and I found ourselves. Of course she and I began to swim. Something had flung us out there. Before we even

thought about it, we were completely immersed in what surrounded us. We had nothing to do with what put us where we
were in the first place; we'd made no decisions.

❖

The greater mystery is why Robert married me. My theory is
that, with varying degrees of understanding, people do know
what's at issue between them. Robert had to know that my
heart was indifferent to him. He chose me anyway. How could I
not take that as clear evidence that he desired to be bound to an
indifferent heart?

❖

A day of audacious sunlight — sunlight as they don't make it
anymore. Ha! Canoeing — the comedy of a dozen girls in half a
dozen boats. And crafts — mind-numbing crafts, a comedy of a
different sort. Next, two hours of free time. Most of the girls
used it for strip poker in the farthest cabin; the counselor there
allowed those games.

So Louise and I found ourselves reading in our cabin. We had
it to ourselves. Outside were the green leaves, barely moving in
the sunlight. The birds were quiet in the hot afternoon.

"Listen to this." I broke the silence. I was reading *Madame
Bovary*, which had an effect on me that I now understand was
mildly disturbing but also pleasurable. At the time, I knew it
only as guilty nervousness with some slight waves of prickling
up my arms. I began reading . . .

As I read, Louise moved idly over to my bunk, climbed across
me with her long legs, and lay down beside me.

I have to repeat that sentence. *As I read, Louise moved idly over
to my bunk, climbed across me with her long legs, and lay down
beside me.* Nothing in all my life was so utterly dear as that.

I did keep reading, of course. Has anyone ever looked into the erotic dimension of reading as an adolescent activity? Not that I recommend it be examined. Leave them alone, poor adolescent girls. Let them be. I was a girl reading a book on a summer afternoon.

This is a little marriage parable. From almost the beginning, Robert announced to our family and friends that he and I had agreed not to have children. In fact, we never discussed the matter. In fact, I've always felt that if anything could have saved me, it would have been my having a child. But I wouldn't tell him that. That I certainly would not give to Robert.

She listened while I read. This for a long time. No one disturbed us. The two of us had the words from the book and sunlit leaves outside, visible through the wire screens on every side of the cabin. We had the fragrance of woods and damp earth and the baked-lumber smell of the inside of the cabin, camper smells, suntan lotion, clean and soiled clothes, and shampoo. I fancy that among the full amalgamation of aromas, I could discern the exact scent of Louise beside me — and, furthermore, that I have transported that scent through time and have it with me now, a permanent possession, a smell I associate with Louise's long legs and the tan shorts she wore that afternoon. What, I ask you, is more incorrigible than romantic memory?

Robert and the Girl — that's the book I should write sometime. Yes, of course I knew. No, I didn't know, certainly not. Either could be true. The girl was Patricia Bunkleman's daughter. Well, she was Calvert Bunkleman's daughter, too, though to everyone except his broker, Calvert was an invisible person — especially to his daughter. But what I "knew" was that, from toddlerhood on, Marcy had an intoxicating effect on Robert. After one of our visits to the Bunklemans', Robert spoke about one thing and another with great energy, until he finally steered the conversation toward the child. I learned to recognize when he wanted me to say things about her and to ask him questions about her. I did that. It wasn't difficult. Marcy was interesting to me, too, but I couldn't keep a conversation going with her. With me, she stood away, kept her distance. It was as if she wanted to observe me without having to interact. I didn't object to her attention in that way; I rather enjoyed it. And it was her mother I liked talking with, anyway. Patricia Bunkleman looked like Louise Harding. Ever so slightly, she was my Louise, grown into a sensible and wryly cheerful woman. That was reason enough for me not to mind the child's studious eyes. And not to mind Robert's cleverly guiding our conversations toward the topic of Marcy.

Sometimes I ask myself whether Robert knew what was happening to him as that child grew up. He wasn't — isn't — the kind of man who would choose to involve himself in an illicit passion. When I thought about it, I admired him for having that element in his character — whether or not he was aware of it.

I can give the particulars to you. But you must understand that these matters — translated into mere language — do not convey what transpired that afternoon. There is no god in these details, though perhaps one hovers not very far away.

Because Louise was beside me, I softened my voice. It wasn't a whisper, because it came from down in my chest, but it wasn't what I used for speaking to people. I may have used it to mur-

mur to myself in, say, a crowded hallway at school. But I had never read aloud with it, never used it with the intention of being heard by anyone. I discovered this voice to be an expressive instrument. With it, I could *sing* — though very softly — those sentences from the book. And as I read, I could feel Louise responding to my voice, though she must also have been caught up in Emma Bovary's story as well.

We rearranged ourselves in the little bunk. We did so with no aim beyond getting comfortable. And since Louise turned on her side toward me, it was perfectly natural that she let her hand rest on my side. I turned a little toward her, too, and then went on reading, not thinking very much about the rearrangement of our bodies.

This is almost too intricate to explain. Marcy Bunkleman did not resemble those qualities of her mother which resembled Louise Harding's. Had they been paintings, Patricia and Louise would have been Renoirs, whereas Marcy would have been a Klimt. Everything about Marcy was definite — her features, her clothes, her way of speaking. I don't know how she is as an adult, but as a child, she knew her own mind. That was the quality that most appealed to Robert. I found it unsettling.

I had only to continue reading, and Louise and I could go on exactly as we were. With my voice sounding out the sentences of the book, I could hold the afternoon still. I could excuse our cabin from the passing of time. It was like singing a painting. The place where I held us with my voice was absolutely our own. So gradually did Louise's hand make its way to my breast that I noticed it only after I realized that what I felt must have been her thumb and fingers lightly moving in time to the words I spoke. I had almost thought it my body's response to what I was reading. I'm certain Louise intended nothing seductive by what her hand did, at least no more than I intended my reading aloud to be a seduction.

There did come a moment, however, when I paused in my reading and looked into my friend's face, which was so close to my own that not to kiss her would have been the more difficult act. So I did. I kissed Louise. A playful kiss that we both let linger until we weren't playing anymore. I knew nothing about kissing — nor, apparently, did she. But in the lingering of it, I had to accept the sexual nature of our situation — though I had only the most basic understanding of sexuality. At any rate, in her rueful smile, which gradually appeared when I opened my eyes to her again, I saw that Louise, too, accepted it.

A length of time passed in our silent gazing at each other.

Finally, she whispered, "Again? Can we do that again, please?"

"I think I should read some more," I whispered.

Neither of us moved.

"All right, then," Louise murmured, staying where she was, hardly even blinking, she was so still. "Go ahead and read."

So we kissed again.

Whatever illusions Louise and I had held until that afternoon fell away. Though she and I had always thought of ourselves as good girls, naughtiness was quite evident from then on. It came to us as if someone else had set us to the task, as if someone else had required it of us.

I have never thought of myself as other than heterosexual. Thus, whatever deceptions I may have practiced in dealing with

Robert, at least in that regard I was not deceiving him. Or no more than I have deceived myself throughout my life.

I can say this with certainty: Louise Harding is the only female to whom I have ever been sexually attracted.

There was a time when I found my husband sexually attractive. I'm fairly certain of that.

Louise and I liked the kissing. It was sufficient for us. I suppose we did know that there was more and that kissing was only a prelude to what else was possible. But we had no need of anything more. In fact, Louise moved her hand *away* from my breast in order to touch my face. As if we were blind, we traced each other's foreheads and cheeks and ears and noses, lips and chins, and we teased a little — "I can see the inside of your nose" — that kind of thing, and Louise let me touch her closed eyelids with the tip of my tongue. It was too hot for us to want to press against each other very much — too hot, really, for us to think of it, because probably if we'd thought of it, we would have done it. We could have. What seemed to occupy us, however, was our faces, the tips of our fingers, and our murmuring voices. When I think of it now, the time we lay there with each other has a *breadth* to it that is more like days or weeks than the mere few minutes it must have been. That stretching out of the time seems to me a divine kindness.

Robert and I are companions. I've thought about this extensively. We are not *dear* companions, which would be another topic altogether. Very seldom are we *dear* to each other. Rather, I think of us as secret agents assigned by the higher powers to work closely with each other, posing as a married couple. And awaiting further orders. Ha! How about that? While we await those orders, Robert and I are carrying out our assigned duties. *There* is a way for you to think about us.

At Camp Mohican with us that summer was Rachel Stevens, a runty girl who, as a lightning rod attracts bolts of atmospheric electricity, drew the hatred of those around her. Rachel's great sin against her sister campers was that she knew things. She knew things because she read, she observed, and she listened. She must have been hated by her schoolmates at home for years, and she must have hoped finally to be appreciated at Camp Mohican. In her first several days at camp, she did show off quite a bit. She knew the camp rules so well that she could recite them as they applied to any given situation; she knew the camp buildings and craft and recreation areas by name and knew which path to take to get to what place; she knew the daily schedule for the whole week; and she generally possessed enough knowledge of history, literature, math, and current events so that she could have functioned respectably as a college senior. She could hardly help being insufferable. Rachel was barely thirteen, and though her mother had brought her to camp with an array of shampoos, soaps, deodorants, lotions, curlers, and even hair sprays, Rachel's hygienic and cosmetic skills were retarded. She was shy about changing clothes and taking showers. She hated using a deodorant. It wasn't so much that she stank as that she set herself up to be accused of stinking.

To Rachel's credit, she didn't impose herself on anyone; she showed us she could survive without having a single friend among us. It was evident that she was accustomed to the role of social outcast, and though she never said so, her demeanor gave us to understand that she considered most of us to be intellectual and spiritual ninnies. Since she wasn't going to gain our appreciation or friendship, she invited us to despise her.

I didn't, really, but in the first week or so of camp, to secure my own social standing, I pretended that I did.

Then at lunch one afternoon Rachel passed behind me as I was lingering at the table, caught up in the last hundred pages of *Look Homeward, Angel*. "If you're smart," she murmured, "you'll skip the parts where he goes on and on." She had paused on her way to return her tray to the kitchen. My impression was that she hadn't actually turned her head toward me; she'd stopped walking for a moment and spoken her sentence to my general vicinity. So I didn't take my eyes away from the pages in front of me.

"Of course," I said.

Rachel stood still a moment longer. I could almost feel her evaluating my response — which I thought to be quite good, given the circumstances. I had expressed agreement, with some condescension but without insult. I took her silence as approval of what I'd said.

There was *that* between us.

That was the condition of being a teenage reader. During my weeks at Camp Mohican, I couldn't have articulated this, but I've had quite a long time to think about it. In a group of upper-middle-class adolescents, the ratio of non- and occasional readers to truly addicted bookworms is about forty to one. The odd thing about reading is that it generates guilt, especially in the young: you're finding out all these secrets — what people really think and feel and do. Ordinary social intercourse is constructed to conceal the truth of such matters. When you're a kid, and you first start reading grown-up books, it's like looking in a window at night at people who think no one is around.

Rachel and I recognized each other to be readers. I knew she understood that, however much I might pretend to be like the others, I was most essentially like *her*. My unavoidable sister-hood with her made me uneasy, and Rachel knew it. We both knew she had a power over me. How she might use it, I couldn't imagine — and I doubted she could either.

Robert and the Girl. Something in that drama transported me back to Camp Mohican. I didn't understand it at first. I thought it was merely the way Patricia Bunkleman reminded me of Louise Harding. But there was more. It was the outrageous impropriety of what they were doing. Robert was in a state of terror at being found out — by me, especially — but he also discovered within himself a capacity for rapture. During the months of his relationship with the girl, Robert took on a spiritual resonance that moved me. Without wanting to, I found that I knew what he felt. I had so very briefly been in the same state myself — filled with rapture and terror in equal parts.

At first I thought I was hallucinating. There was a face at the screen door to the cabin, but it was sideways and in the bottom corner. Because it was sideways — and because my vision of it was skewed by the angle at which I looked across Louise's neck and ear and hair — it was the face of a gargoyle. As I tried to focus on that part of the screen, with the sunlight and shadows flickering in the background, what I saw became more and more a vision of splotched light, darkness, and color — a Cha-

gall or a Kandinsky. The sideways face seemed to be fixed in a
gleeful grin. For a long while I studied it. Louise's eyes were
closed. She was breathing deeply, asleep or nearly so. I said
nothing.

It gradually came to me. The face was Rachel's.

She was lying on the porch, her head propped on her hand,
looking in at us.

Louise stood three inches taller than I. My view of her included
an expanse of her snowy neck. And that was perfectly all right
with me. Hers was a neck worth remembering.

Once when he returned from Singapore, Robert was invited for
lunch by the Bunklemans. Immediately after he returned home,
he came to our sunroom, where I do my reading. "I have to tell
you about this," he said and sat down opposite me to describe
what had happened.

Patricia had let him in, but she was running late and needed
a shower, and Cal had had to cancel out because of a last-
minute meeting downtown. So Patricia asked Robert to wait in
the living room with Marcy. She would entertain him, Patricia
assured him. At the time, Marcy was thirteen. When Robert
walked in, the girl was standing up, waiting for him and dressed
charmingly, as if for a cotillion. They sat down, rather formally,
he thought. Leaning forward in her chair, she began to interview him. She was specifically interested in — as Robert told me
she phrased it — "girls who played sports" in the Philippines
and the other countries where Robert's business had taken him.
"What kind of girls are they?" she wanted to know. "Do you
mind telling me about them?" It was as if, before voicing it to

Robert that afternoon, she had been worrying the question in her mind for quite a while.

Robert wanted to be able to converse with Marcy intelligently. He thought her manners and appearance suggested that she saw this as an occasion to present herself as a grown-up. Indeed, Robert said, if one went by appearance and manner of speaking, she was as grown up as any woman he'd met. So he confessed to her that he hadn't a clue about female athletes in his own country, let alone the Philippines. "But I'm very interested in why this question concerns you, Marcy," he said. "Something about your own experience must have brought it to mind."

They looked at each other for a moment, until Robert saw that she was blushing. He started to apologize, but she interrupted him. "No, it's all right," she said. "I was just trying to analyze myself. I think I'm worried about what kind of girl I am — or what kind of girl I'll be — if I stay on the track team."

"You love running, I know that," Robert said. He knew that Marcy, all through middle school, had been a champion runner.

"Yes," she said. "I do love it. But this year all the girls who were my friends have stopped caring about it. The ones who care about it now are . . . I don't know how to put it."

"You don't have anything in common with them?" Robert offered.

Marcy smiled and nodded, but she cast her eyes down modestly. She straightened herself and slightly rearranged her hands and feet in the classic pose of good posture.

Robert understood then that she really wanted to know what he thought of her. She had never before presented herself to him as a young woman. He understood, furthermore, that for her this conversation was not a casual one, nor was the question. *He* had been designated as the person to tell her, at this point in her life, whether or not she would be considered an attractive young woman. Robert said that it was all he could do not to blurt out something ridiculous like "Hey, kid, don't worry, you look great." But he knew that what the occasion called for — and what she truly needed — was for him to address her as an adult.

"Marcy, I hope this won't embarrass you," he said, "but my guess is that there aren't many people at your school who can recognize your kind of beauty. You're going to have to be patient with them. When you get to college, you'll find people who will appreciate you, people who have an eye for a woman who's truly beautiful. You're just going to have to wait a while."

I told Robert that what he'd said to Marcy was perfectly appropriate, and he nodded his thanks to me.

"I thought so, too," he said. "At any rate, she seemed to consider my advice for several moments before she cleared her throat and raised an eyebrow. 'Four years,' she said. 'Approximately one third of my lifetime so far.'"

I had to choose whether or not to tell Louise that Rachel had seen us. I knew it would spoil everything. I could envision Louise's face as I spoke, as she began to find me repulsive — because of our being seen by the despicable Rachel. So of course I didn't tell her. I never did.

One afternoon Rachel found me alone. She knew I had a special place to read, in the big assembly room, which was never used for anything but whole camp assemblies. She came up beside me and sat down and began speaking. She and I were sitting in metal folding chairs, looking very nearly straight ahead; I was pretending not to listen to her, and she was pretending to be telling her story, not to me, but to the air around us, to the empty room.

Last year a boy at school kissed me. I accidentally saw him kick a dent in the door of a car in the teachers' parking lot. He turned and saw me looking at him. Like a little dance, he demonstrated the kicking move for me again, something he must have seen in the movies. I didn't say anything. I wanted to run, but I didn't. That boy was maybe a couple of years older than me, and I was scared of him. He walked right up to me and touched my shoulder with his finger. "See, I won't hurt you," he said, but he didn't smile. I was afraid to move, because he was staring at me. Then he kissed me, a hard, bumping kind of kiss, with one hand holding my shoulder. "I might let you go to bed with me when you get older," he said. And he walked away.

What I was to make of that little parable, I didn't know — and still don't. But I'm certain that Rachel had thought about it most carefully before she recited it to me. Very likely she made it up. I suspect her of that, but I'm not certain. Real or made-up, it was nevertheless something she chose to give me.

From her earliest memory, Louise had been close to her grandmother. Mom Harding liked nothing more than taking Louise shopping and buying her whatever she liked. It was a tradition — once a month on Saturday morning, her mother dropped her off, and her grandmother drove the two of them downtown. The Hardings lived in Cincinnati. Mom Harding and Louise had lunch at Bronson's and spent the rest of the afternoon cruising through the department stores they both loved. Louise said that when she was around ten, her grandmother informed her that the two of them looked alike, an idea that at first seemed preposterous to her because their ages were so different. But, Louise said, she did see a resemblance in their coloring, their skin, their eyes, even their hair, which wasn't at all the same but which Louise could imagine as being the same before her grandmother's hair turned gray. Louise said it nearly freaked her out, *understanding* how her grandmother had once looked just like her — or how, in fifty years, she was going to look like her grandmother.

When Louise turned eleven, her grandmother bought her a cocktail dress. They went to Martel's, a small shop where her grandmother had done business for many years. The ladies there helped them pick out a petite navy blue dress that was sophisticated but also, somehow, looked all right for a child. Louise said that both she and her grandmother were so proud of their purchase that they cut short their afternoon and drove directly to Louise's house to show it to her mother. The grandmother insisted that Louise go straight upstairs, put on the dress, and come down to model it for her mother. Louise said that as she stepped in proud circles with the dress on, she noticed her mother blushing and acting somewhat constrained in her conversation with the grandmother — her mother-in-law. She didn't, however, really realize anything was wrong until her grandmother had left the house and her mother informed her that the dress had to be returned immediately. The mother spent the whole drive back into downtown Cincinnati explaining to Louise that she could not appropriately wear a dress like that for another four or five years.

The cocktail dress purchase apparently was the first in a series of strange acts by the grandmother. On what was supposed to be another regular Saturday afternoon shopping trip to downtown Cincinnati, Mom Harding drove the two of them all the way to Louisville and checked into a hotel before she suggested that Louise call home to tell her parents where they were. Louise didn't know whether her grandmother had planned that journey or had simply thought it up as they set out for their usual shopping tour. At any rate, she enjoyed seeing Louisville with her grandmother, and that was a good thing, because it was the last outing she and her grandmother were allowed to take alone. From then on, Louise's mother or father accompanied them on their shopping trips. Not very long after that, Louise's father had to take Mom Harding's car away from her. And last year she had to move into a special home.

The grandmother's most recent phase of odd behavior was — and Louise confessed her delight in it as a regrettable perversity of her own — utterly fascinating. As much as it was within her power to be so, Mom Harding was a family outlaw. She escaped supervision whenever possible. She simply walked away from anybody who was with her and disappeared — and she was very sly about it. Sometimes she couldn't be found, and she wouldn't turn up for hours. Louise's parents once "lost" the grandmother overnight and never did find out where she'd gone or how she'd spent that time.

"Just before I came here," Louise told me, "my mother and I went to the home so that we could take Mom Harding out to this restaurant for lunch. When the waiter brought the check, my mother put the money for it on the little tray that held it; then she went to the ladies' room. I should have known better than to leave my grandmother at the table by herself, but I got up and walked around to look at some pictures on the walls of the restaurant. I happened to glance back at our table just as Mom Harding picked up the tray and slipped it into her big purse — tray, check, and money, the whole thing. I saw her watching the ladies' room door for my mother, and I tried to turn away before she looked over at me. It didn't work — she caught me catching her. Just as my mother appeared and headed back to our table, Mom Harding's eyes met mine. She knew I knew what she had done. She gave me this grim little smile, but she didn't take the stuff out of her purse."

Louise hushed and looked at me with a ghost of a smile.

"What did you do?" I asked.

"What would you have done?" she asked in return.

I insisted that she finish the story.

"Well, my choices were pretty clear," Louise said. "Tell or don't tell. It had to be one or the other, didn't it?"

I refused to answer; I looked away.

"To tell you the truth, I wasn't sure what I was going to do. The three of us walked out of the restaurant, and I kept waiting for the maître d' or the waiter or somebody to stop us. Nobody did. We got in the car, with me in the back seat, and Mom Harding turned and gave me another one of those little smiles that was at least half grimace. I really tried to make myself lean forward and tell my mother before we got out of the parking lot, but I couldn't. Mom Harding must have understood that after we were on the road I wasn't going to tell on her. So the next time she looked back at me, the look on her face surprised me. It was almost as if she was feeling sorry for me — as if she thought I *should* have told my mother but I hadn't and so now where was I?"

Since it seemed to me that Louise had not finished telling the story, I didn't say anything. I waited for her to go on.

"You don't understand, do you?" she said.

"I guess I don't," I said.

"I couldn't really be on my grandmother's side, because I wasn't a little girl anymore; she knew that. But I wasn't on my mother's side either, or I would have told her; Mom Harding knew that, too. She looked at me, in the back seat, the way you'd look at somebody locked up in a prison cell."

She stopped again.

"What are you trying to tell me?" I asked.

"What I just told you," she said. "A story about my grandmother." And she looked at me in a way that must have been a demonstration of how her grandmother had looked at her in the car that day.

Robert and I had lunched with old friends out at Shaker Point. We'd said our good-byes and were out in the parking lot when we encountered Patricia and Marcy on their way in. The four of us exchanged polite kisses. I had to ask about Cal, and Patricia had to offer up the usual intricate excuse for his not being with them. There was nothing unusual about it, of course. Cal was never in the company of his wife and daughter if he could avoid it, but we all had to pretend that he was a martyr to his work, a noble and long-suffering man. My mind tended to wander whenever Patricia carried out one of these tedious explanations. In this case my eyes also wandered briefly. Marcy stood with her eyes cast down and with her hands lightly clasped in front of her blue sundress. In the bright August sunlight, she was so astoundingly pretty that I had to ask myself how I could not have remarked it before. Of course the answer was that she was fourteen years old. She had suddenly slipped out of childhood. In her possession, during those late summer months, were an exact purity of skin and an elegance of bone and muscle around her shoulders and arms. It also occurred to me, noting how she seemed lost in her own thoughts, that she may have been trying to make herself invisible to Robert and me. I almost laughed aloud at the absurdity of the thought, that Marcy was like some bird or animal whose deepest wish was to camouflage herself, to disappear into her surroundings, but who — in the glare of the parking lot — was an almost unbearably vivid spectacle.

Then I glanced at Robert. His eyes were on Marcy — how could they have been seeing anything else? — and they were widened, like those of a startled horse. In the moment, he too seemed to me a great joke — *Man Aflame in Sunlit Parking Lot.* I imagined interrupting Patricia's interminable monologue by murmuring to him, "Do you think she's pretty, Robert?"

My amusement, however, ceased when I realized that I could no longer merely suspect something transpiring between Robert and Marcy. Certainty, whether or not I wanted it, had arrived.

Rachel, that little watcher, found a way to confront Louise and me. I suppose it wasn't so difficult for her to see where we went, because Louise and I had taken to slipping away during free time and meandering down the back way to Lake Mohican. It was a walk of maybe fifteen minutes that, in our jostling and stopping to tease each other and talk, Louise and I usually stretched out to half an hour. Though we never kissed on those walks — we never, in fact, kissed again after the one time together in our cabin — we held hands or strolled with our arms around each other's waist and our hips lightly bumping. Later, when I thought about how Rachel may have spied on us in our intimacy, I cringed. Where the path came out was a cleared area, with a picnic table perfectly placed for a view of the lake down through a corridor of trees.

This particular afternoon I had my heart set on engaging

Louise in a conversation about our feelings for each other. During our hundreds of hours of talking, we had confessed to each other secrets about ourselves and our families, but we hadn't ever talked about our immediate circumstances. I was shy about saying anything directly to Louise about my caring for her, and I suppose it was the same for her.

You understand, I never had the slightest doubt about Louise's devotion to me or mine to her. Even if we hadn't spoken the words, the truth of our feelings wasn't an issue. I knew she loved me as surely as I knew the picnic table would be at the end of the path, as surely as I knew there would be trees and a lake, sunlight and shadow, when we reached our quiet place.

As was our custom, we sat down across from each other. I reached for her hands, and she opened them to me.

That was when Rachel stepped out of the woods, walked to our table, and sat down — at the other end, on the side where I was but a couple of feet away, and facing Louise.

As I thought about it later, I understood that Rachel hadn't really been hiding; she'd placed herself so that, had we been alert, we would have seen her standing at the edge of the trees. But we had been so absorbed in each other that we'd taken no note of her. That may well have incensed her, and it probably gave her the nerve to act as she did. She never looked directly at us. She seated herself carefully in her place at the table, folded her hands before her, and studied them through her thick glasses.

"You're dirty," she said. "You two are dirty."

Her voice was so uneven that I could clearly hear her fear. I knew how desperately her heart must have been thumping as she forced herself to say those words while staring at her grossly chewed thumbnails. But I wasn't looking at Rachel; I was studying Louise's face, directly across from mine. Her eyes were on Rachel. To me, it was a terrible sight, because if Rachel had slapped Louise as hard as she could, forehand and backhand across the face, she couldn't have hurt her more than she did with those two brief sentences. Louise flinched; tears welled up in her eyes; and her lips opened, though she made no sound. What I felt for her at that moment nearly made my heart explode. And that was when Louise turned her eyes to me, as if to ask, "Is she right? Are we really dirty?"

My blood raced through my veins. I made a noise that wasn't language at all. Then I was standing and moving toward the circle of stones around a blackened piece of ground. I felt huge. I picked up a stone nearly the size of my head — one far too heavy for me to lift, but I lifted it easily — lifted it above my head, and turned back to the table, to Rachel, whom I so deeply hated, whose wretched face I hated so much! I stood before her and smashed down the stone — onto the table directly in front of her.

The timber of the table cracked, and the two girls screamed. They kept screaming for some moments. Rachel's face was awful. Her hands jumping to her face had knocked off her glasses. She scrambled up from the table, staring at me the whole time, and began running.

"Rachel!" my voice rang out.

As if I'd threatened to shoot her unless she halted where she was, she stopped running.

I picked up her glasses from the ground beside the table and slowly carried them to her. "You forgot these." I handed them to her, and she took them and stood there, sobbing.

"You can go now," I told her. "But don't run. Walk all the way back."

When Rachel had been out of sight for at least a minute, I

looked at Louise. She must have been watching my back the whole time. "My God, Suzanne," she murmured.

I wanted to sit beside her and put my arms around her. I wanted to hold her, and I wanted her to hold me. I wanted to fall back with her into the great sweet lap of timelessness. But her face said that it would never happen again.

So you see, there is really no way around this — what shall we call it? — this *episode*. Nothing accounts for it; nothing explains it. I come from a long line of educated and responsible people. Except for that three-minute blip in my history, I have been an even-tempered — even *placid,* to use Robert's word for me — person. Yes, I avoid conflict. No, I do not stand up for myself. Yes, I have been deceived and treated shabbily, and yes, rage must lie smoldering somewhere inside me. But no, I am not likely now or in the future to do anything about it.

Robert very nearly threw me over a cliff. He could have done it and gotten away with it. And do you know what I felt? I felt *empathy!* In the actual moment when I thought it was about to happen, a voice in me was goading him on, was encouraging him. *"Yes! Do it! Take the girl!"*

9

News

IT PLEASES my mother to remember the news of Robert's death before the end of our weekly Sunday afternoon telephone conversation. She gives me the details — a stroke hit him in the lobby of his office building; he'd just turned seventy-three; he'd only recently agreed to retire; Suzanne is holding up very well . . . Part of my mind keeps up with her. When I ask about the funeral, she seems to relish telling me there will not be one; instead, there will be a memorial service. She sounds as if she's proud of Robert for requesting cremation.

Somewhere I've seen pictures of how they do it. A sort of trolley moves the body into the furnace.

I thank my mother for remembering to tell me the news. As always, whenever his name comes up in our conversations, I consider telling her about "the adventure" Robert and I had when I was fifteen; she's consistently been so smug about her friendship with him. But it would be pure meanness for me to tell her that now. She's just his age. She could have a stroke this minute, while she's talking with me on the phone. So I lead her through our closing rituals. "Yes, yes, Suellen's here this weekend, and she's taking very good care of me. Next Sunday, if not before. Right. Love you, too. Good-bye, Mother." I'm grateful Suellen's out of the house, so that I can embrace this silence and the late afternoon sunlight angling through my living room windows. I sit still and wait for the rage I know is coming. I'm ready to take hold of it.

But such sorrow for Robert keeps welling up in me that I am ashamed. More than anything, he wanted me to love him, and of course I never did. Childish as I was in so many ways, at least I never fooled myself about that. Why, then, am I grieving for him now? I lecture myself — the man was arrogant; he was vain; he was selfish . . . But I can't stop the sadness I feel for him. I can't change it or do anything except let it keep coming. Before I finish crying, I start laughing, too, a little bitterly, because I realize I don't have to answer to anyone. Who cares what I feel — except me? Suellen is here this weekend, helping me prepare to sell the house, but she's out in the storage room above the garage, sifting through papers and junk. I have this sorrow all to myself, and even though it isn't the emotion I want, it is, nevertheless, something clear and true that I can feel about Robert. So I'm glad for it.

I sit watching the deepening light through my windows. Out there, it's midsummer and so hot that I have to keep the air conditioning on day and night. The house is cool, but because it's sealed off from outside noise, it feels almost institutional. When my children were growing up, this room would never have been so quiet. Like their father, Erin and Suellen took pleasure in using their voices. And of course there was always the sound of the TV in the family room, a ringing phone, boom boxes from their bedrooms, or a raucous conversation between Allen and one or both of them in the kitchen. Allen himself never hesitates to replace silence with words.

Like a rock thrown through the window, it comes to me: no Robert, no Allen.

Robert prepared me for Allen. In those long ago days, if I'd been an ordinary fifteen-year-old girl, Allen Crandall would have intimidated me. He made no secret about thinking that he was smarter than most of his teachers, so I'd have been put off by his aggressive ways, and he'd have found me childish. But when I became Robert's lover, half of me instantly grew up. Half child and half adult, I wasn't like anybody my age. It was because he was so brash that Allen appealed to me. And because I'd just discovered that I held the power to make Robert do whatever I wanted him to, I had unshakable confidence in myself. Unlike every other kid in our school, I wasn't even slightly afraid of Allen, and he found that attractive.

I've always prided myself on having broken with Robert cleanly and completely, with no help from anyone. And I'm not ready now to see that man as having held my life in his hands all this time without my knowing it. As Suellen would put it, "That's harsh, Mom." That's what she'd say if she were to come inside now and I informed her that I've just understood that she owes her very existence to a dead man named Robert Gordon.

Hardly any daylight is left, but I have no desire to turn on the lights in the living room. My life has caved in on me. I sit where I am and wonder whether I'll ever again want to move.

10

Silk Dress

My mother has turned to stone. That's the first thought that
occurs to me when I bring in the dress to show her. After I
switch on the table lamp in the hallway, I'm startled to see her
sitting in the dark living room. I've never seen her so still. Then
I really do become frightened as I walk toward her, because
she isn't quick to come back to herself. *She's not old enough to
have a stroke* is my next thought. When I see her face, it's as
if she's aging right before my eyes. I can hardly stand the look
she gives me, sadness so deep, it's as if it came from the bottom of a grave to take hold of her. I'm glad I have the silk dress
to show her and take her mind off her troubles. "Okay, Mom,"
I say, "what's the story here? I found this way down at the
bottom of that trunk in the garage. It doesn't look like any of
your other old clothes. Or any of your new ones, either, for that
matter."

I love her face then. My mother's face when she's happy — or
about to be happy, that moment just before it comes to her — is
almost my deepest wish. She doesn't get up, but she reaches for
the dress, takes it from me, and runs her hands over it as if it's
something she lost a long time ago.

"See how it's stained here?" she says, pointing to what I'd already noticed. She shakes her head, still smiling, though a little grimly now. She gazes at the dress in her lap and strokes it, without saying anything, for a long while. Then she does begin to speak.

"I was an athlete, Suellen." My mother glances at me and pauses, as if to be sure she's telling it right. She starts again. "I was on the track team, and people all over the city knew about me. Being a runner meant a great deal to me — it was how the teachers and the other students thought of me. So the whole time I was a teenager, getting dressed up wasn't the same thing for me that it was for most girls my age. I thought buying an expensive dress to wear once to a dance was a stupid thing to do.

"My sophomore year was when I began dating your father. He understood my attitude toward dressing up. Mostly it didn't matter to him, and he enjoyed teasing me about some of the things I chose to wear to school. 'Farm girl,' he liked to call me, or 'the hippie chick.' The one time it did matter to him — his senior prom — he made it clear that he expected me to get 'gussied up,' as he called it.

"After we were down at U.Va., I began to see that he had an attitude about how I looked in a dress. He liked it when a fraternity brother gave me the once-over or let out a low whistle. And he laughed when he caught me blushing over that kind of male behavior. Nowadays when I remember some of the things your father said about my appearance before we were married, I can't imagine how I put up with him. Back then, though, he seemed to me both liberal and manly.

"My twenty-first birthday fell on the last Saturday of October. Your father wanted to make a big deal out of it. I was in my last semester of nursing school, and he'd just started working in

Washington. He planned to drive down to Charlottesville on Friday morning, pick me up, and then drive the two of us all the way up to New York. You can imagine what a totally ridiculous drive that was, but he liked to make grand gestures in those days. He'd reserved rooms for us at the Plaza. There was a revival of *Our Town* that he was going to buy tickets for, and he was going to make late reservations at an Italian restaurant where the waiters and bartenders sang opera arias while they served dinner. When your father told me over the phone about the singing waiters, he actually sang a few bars of his idea of opera music.

"'I get the idea,' I told him. 'And I'll be able to think about it a lot more clearly if you just let me imagine how they do it in the restaurant.'

"But I really felt torn. Of course I was touched that your father wanted to make an occasion out of my birthday, but it seemed too much trouble. I had school and floor duty to deal with, and, to be really petty about it, the man wanted to pick me up at the break of dawn on one of the rare mornings of the school year when I could sleep in. I was on the verge of telling him to forget the traveling and the fancy entertainment and just come to Charlottesville, sing a corny happy birthday to me, and take me out to dinner.

"Then my mother — to whom your father had confided his plans — sent down the dress.

"It was a white silk sheath, and it was the only piece of clothing I've ever held in my hands that I simply couldn't resist trying on. In my dorm room, by myself, I took it out of the box and held it up to myself in front of the mirror. I could hardly put it on fast enough. Feeling sleek and light as a dove, I was too excited to stand in the room by myself, so I stepped out into the hall and shouted, 'Hey, everybody, come check this out!' Up and down the corridor, girls drifted casually out of their rooms and then stood there, gawking. I watched their faces.

"What I saw was their opinion that almost anybody who put on that dress could instantly become beautiful.

"I was so impatient to talk to Allen that I went ahead and used the telephone at the end of our dormitory hallway, which was how the phone set-up was in those days. 'I've made my decision,' I told him. I forced myself not to tell him about the dress.

"To wear white silk in New York City — that was my daydream as I went to my classes and did my shifts in the hospital. When I walked into the singing restaurant, everybody would turn and stare. The best part of all would be when one of those musical waiters — the most handsome in the whole place — went down on one knee and opened his arms toward me and began to sing, 'O Beautiful Lady in the White Silk Dress!'

"But wouldn't you know it would rain? It also turned out to be the particular fall morning in Charlottesville when the weather turns chilly. My alarm woke me up while it was still dark outside, and then your father was late picking me up. In the car, he and I fell into a pissy argument over which of us caused the other the most inconvenience. We bickered from northern Virginia up into Pennsylvania. All the way up the East Coast it rained steadily. And of course we had to get lost driving into the city. When we finally pulled up in front of the Plaza, instead of being filled with joy and wonder, I felt like a street urchin asking for a handout. I didn't get all that wet, just moving from the car to the front entrance, but I felt so bedraggled that I might as well have been drenched. When I stepped inside and got a look at the lobby's chandeliers and deep carpets and five-thousand-dollar sofas, I wanted to turn around and walk right back out to the car. The doorman, the desk clerk, and the bellboy all seemed to be snotty to us, though I'm not sure if they really were or if we were being paranoid. At any rate, your father became deeply pouty. In the elevator, going up to our rooms, making a show of looking at his watch, he informed me that we were too late to make the play.

"'If we hadn't made that wrong turn when we came up out of the tunnel,' he said. Of course I knew what he meant was that *I* had said we had to get in the right lane to be headed toward the Plaza. Why didn't he just say it straight out: 'This is all your fault, Marcy'?

"When I was finally alone in my room, I locked the door, swore to myself I wasn't leaving it until breakfast the next morning, and took to my bed.

"But once I was lying down in that quiet place, I got to thinking about your father. Everybody has bad moments; surely he was entitled to a few. I guessed that I had just seen one of his worst. But there was something else about him in this situation for me to consider. He had taken separate rooms for us. This was still in the late sixties, mind you. When everybody else was rebelling like crazy, your father had it in him to be old-fashioned. Seducing me was not one of his goals. If it had been up to me, it would have been fine for the two of us to stay in the same room in order to save money. But I appreciated your father for seeing it his own way.

"Somebody knocking on the door woke me from a deep sleep. Taking a nap was the first thing I did in my room at the Plaza, and whatever else I may have to say about that hotel, I have to testify that those beds, with their crisp and scented linens, were ideal for a little snooze. I'd had the world's greatest nap.

"It was your father at the door, of course. After I was sufficiently awake, I knew he had to be the one. I had to remind my-

self how mad he'd made me. 'Go away!' I yelled at the door. I
was half kidding, but I thought the man ought to know he had
some paying to do before he'd be back in my good graces.

"It was quiet out there for so long that I thought he'd finally
gone. I was even starting to feel a little wretched about telling
him to go away. When the knocking started up again — a very
soft tapping — I knew what his gentle knocking on the door
was telling me. 'I'm sorry,' it said. 'Please forgive me. I promise I
won't act like a jackass anymore. I'll be good.'

"He made me smile. First I put on my bathrobe. *Then* I
opened the door.

"Your father was standing at the threshold, all dressed up and
holding a huge bouquet of red roses. There were twenty-one of
them, but I thought I must be seeing at least fifty. He had asked
the hotel for a vase, so the roses were flared out in front of him.
It looked as if his chest and shoulders had been changed into
gorgeous red blossoms.

"'Oooohhh,' I heard myself saying. Your father was saying it,
too, making the same sound I did, as if he'd been standing out
there just crazy with wanting me to open up the door and see
what he'd brought me.

"In this very apologetic voice, he explained that he'd changed
our dinner reservations to an earlier time. I was still too full of
surprise and pleasure to say anything, but I stood aside and
made a little gesture for him to come into the room. He tiptoed
by me, carrying the vase of flowers, and it took him a moment
or two to decide to put it on the table by the windows. By then
I'd regained some composure. While we looked at the roses in
their place, I could feel myself blushing with pleasure at what
your father had done. I was extremely aware of his presence in
my room, and I thought I should be careful not to let him see

how sentimental he'd made me feel, so I asked him to wait for me in the lobby.

"'All right, Marcy,' he said in this very soft voice. I could tell that his remorse had made him vulnerable. That was when I decided to make a little show for him, of myself in the white dress. I was curious to see if I could move him — to see if I could make him feel as helpless as he'd made me feel with those roses.

"As I say, getting dressed up wasn't something I had much experience doing, and I had nobody there to advise me. I decided not to attempt eye shadow or mascara. I did risk dabbing on a little lipstick. Also, to help me get ready for this trip, Uta had taught me a way to put up my hair that, she said, would look exactly right with the dress.

"Downstairs, when I stepped out of the elevator, I saw that your father had found a little section of the lobby where he could sit more or less by himself. I took a deep breath, raised my shoulders, and walked toward him.

"He didn't know who I was! He stood up — and it was for a stranger that he got to his feet. By the time I reached him, it had broken through to him who the woman in the white dress was — and he'd put his face straight. I'd seen enough, though, to be certain he hadn't known who was walking toward him when he first stood up.

"What he did next was to open his arms, a gesture so untypical of your father that I didn't immediately move into them. Instead, I caught his arms with my hands at his elbows — and locked us into a pose somewhere between an embrace and a shove. With the two of us fixed as we were, I looked up at his face to see what it would tell me.

"He was blinking. It was evident that my seeing his face right then wasn't what he wanted. 'You're very beautiful,' he murmured. Perhaps I should have taken that compliment as the applause I wanted for my little show. But I kept holding him away with my arms and looking up at him.

"I understood that his saying I was beautiful wasn't a lie at all; he was acknowledging what the dress had done to me. But it was also a yelp, a flinching away. Your father thought he knew the person he was about to marry, and then she walked up to him, looking like someone else. He thought he was marrying one person; now it was clear he was marrying at least two. He must have wondered who else — what new stranger with my face and my body — was going to come striding toward him when he was sitting down and minding his own business.

"To anybody watching us, our pose must have been comical. We finally did complete the embrace. I moved all the way into his arms, but my timing was wrong, and I felt awkward. When we moved apart, I could instantly sense a change in him. He'd taken on new energy and poise. He helped me with my coat, offered me his arm as we walked across the lobby to the Plaza's main exit, and chatted up the doorman as the man was summoning a taxi for us. And in the taxi, he was attentive to me, witty, at ease, and talkative with the driver. He radiated so much energy that I congratulated myself for how my dress had affected him.

"In the anteroom of Uccello's, when I took off my coat, I felt as if a spotlight was shining on me and following me into the dining room. No one got down on his knees to sing to me, but the maître d' and the waiters spoke quietly and respectfully to us. And my wish came true: people at tables all over the restaurant turned to watch us walk to our table. It was so scary that I couldn't imagine how I'd thought being stared at by a hundred strangers would be fun. I made a new wish — that this was the last time it would ever happen to me.

"At U.Va., your father was known as the man who never drank more than one beer an evening. He was no drinker, and I certainly wasn't. As a child I'd promised your great-grandfather that I wouldn't have a single alcoholic drink until I was twenty-one. My first sip of Chianti that night at Uccello's tasted better than anything I'd had in all my life.

"Maybe it was a little touristy, but the restaurant was very exciting. The waiters sang; the bartenders sang. There was even a huge woman with a red face who came out of the kitchen, with a cook's uniform on, took off her chef's hat, and sang a glorious aria from *The Marriage of Figaro*. At the end, all the waiters joined in. They were basses and tenors and baritones, and she was this powerful soprano soaring way up above all the other voices.

"Your father stood up to applaud the great soprano, and I reached for the table to steady it. As I did that, I tipped over my wine glass, and your father lunged for it. He did catch it, in fact, but when he slapped his hand around the glass, the wine sloshed out in my direction. In that crazy collaboration, he and I spilled most of a full glass of Chianti down the front of my dress. We froze exactly as we were and stared at the red splash down my front.

"I still believe it wasn't the wine I'd drunk that made me do what I did next. It had to be the spell of the dress. When I could finally let go of staring down at the red on white, I heard myself utter this little anguished cry as I got up and started moving. Awkward in my high heels, I ran through the tables of diners, who gaped at me from all sides.

"Inside the ladies' room, I went to the row of sinks. I didn't think. I didn't hesitate. I got out of that dress so fast I almost ripped it. I had to do something immediately, so I stuffed it into the sink and ran a blast of cold water on it.

"Standing there, rinsing out the white silk, wearing my half slip, French bra, underpants, white stockings and garter belt, and heels — everything white, bought by my mother to go with the dress — I happened to glance up and see myself in the mirror.

"My dress was soaking wet. Just exactly what was I going to do?

"A thin, older woman stepped into the ladies' room, took in the sight, and quickly moved toward the stalls. When she came out, I tried to meet her eyes, but she wouldn't look at me and didn't pause on her way out.

"Two more women who came in refused to talk to me. I wanted to call them snooty New York bitches to their faces, but of course I didn't. The fourth woman who came in was, I later learned, from Texas; she was curious, chatty, and maybe a little drunk. She called me honey and made me repeat the story of the dress's getting stained before she agreed to go into the dining area and find Allen. She had him fetch my coat from the check room and give it to her. And then, as if she was giving me a present, she carried it into the ladies' room. When I asked her what I could do to thank her, she said, 'Oh, honey, you've already given me something to tell those people back in Fort Worth. You take good care now.' She gave me a boozy hug, and we left the ladies' room together.

"The maître d' brought us a plastic bag for my wet dress. My soaking it had merely changed it from a white dress with a red splash into a generally pink dress with a darker pink stain down the front. It certainly seemed ruined, but what was I going to do? Throw it in the trash? I squeezed it up as small as I could and stuffed the bag into my coat pocket.

"In my big buttoned-up coat, I looked respectable enough in the Uccello anteroom. Neither Allen nor I wanted to go back to our table; we said we'd skip dessert and coffee. The maître d' and our waiter felt terrible about what had happened, so we weren't charged for the wine. 'That wine may have been free, but it was the most expensive wine we'll ever have,' your father murmured to me as we were leaving.

"Out on the street, Allen flagged a taxi. Without saying so to each other, I'm sure we both had the idea of going back to the Plaza. But as soon as I climbed into the cab, I knew that wasn't what I wanted to do. I realized that I was in a mood — a mood like never before. My blood was rocketing through my body. The spell of the dress must have been still working on me, except that now it was the opposite of wearing the dress; it was *not* wearing it that had me feeling a little crazy.

"I wanted something *really* exciting to happen. That's what I whispered to your father. I also told him where I wanted to go. He must have been in a mood, too, because he met my eyes and laughed as if our dinner had been nothing but a good time. And he told the cab driver to take us to the Empire State Building.

"It was a cool October night, but I had to have the windows open. At midtown, we passed crowds of people. Somebody lifted a hand to wave — probably not at our taxi, but that didn't matter to me, because I wanted to wave back. Then I was waving to anybody on the street. I was speaking to people, too. 'Hi, sir, how are you?' and 'Oh, rich lady, I love your hat!' and 'Hey, mister, better find yourself a safe place to sleep tonight.'

"I had this intense awareness of being undressed. Instead of feeling embarrassed or ashamed, I was giddy and full of myself, as if I were pulling some grand prank. I could even see it in the faces of people who met my eyes when we passed them — a kind of gleeful approval. They seemed to know the funny and exciting news that my dress was in my coat pocket.

"Your father's mood wasn't the same as mine, but he was at ease and very tolerant of me. I appreciated that. I think he had put himself in a frame of mind to see this as my birthday night. If I wanted to make an utter fool of myself, well, he could certainly put up with that in a city where no one knew either of us. When we got to the Empire State Building, he gave our cabby a generous tip, and was then very smooth in buying a ticket and moving us into line to ride to the top.

"You know how quiet people are in an elevator, even a big one like that? In the hush after the doors sealed us in, I could hardly keep myself from giggling aloud. Surrounded by all those completely dressed people, I was standing there almost naked. And they didn't know it. That was delicious!

"'I'm hot. I think I'll take my coat off,' I told Allen in a voice loud enough for everyone to hear. He opened his mouth to remind me that I certainly *shouldn't* do that, but then realized I was teasing. He winked and said, 'Go ahead. I'll carry it for you.' His voice was loud, too, and he kept looking at me with a smile. Neither of us gave a glance to anybody else in the elevator.

"He really was in on it with me. He was my fellow conspirator; that made me feel so close to him. In an elevator full of strangers, I had an almost joyful experience with your father.

"Maybe because it had turned cool, it was also a clear night in New York — unusually clear, someone told us at the top when we stepped out to the viewing area. Allen and I moved quickly to the shoulder-high wall where we could look out over the city. Huge space opened out before us. Though there were people behind us and on both sides of us, I lost track of them. As far as I was concerned, your father and I were alone in the dark, sparkling world. Lights were everywhere, and they weren't far away, as I had imagined they would be. They were close enough for me to stretch out my hand and take hold of them. And though there wasn't exactly a wind out there, the air was stirring all around us. It was a silky cold that mildly shocked me by brushing my face and rising up inside my coat.

"Because of the high wall, we couldn't look straight down to the street, so I never had a sense of height. It was more like a place I'd come to in a dream. When Allen asked whether I was cold, I told him that I wasn't. I knew I was *going* to be cold, but it hadn't hit me yet. I turned to thank him for asking — I was even about to confess that I liked the cool air on my skin.

"He was standing with his back against the wall, staring toward the elevators.

"'Don't you want to see the lights?' I said.

"'No,' he said. He gave me a little smile, but his voice sounded pinched, a little shrill. Then I noticed that his forehead was wet. It flashed into my mind that maybe he'd caught something; maybe he had a fever.

"'Are you all right?' I asked.

"He said he was, and he turned his face away. His behavior was so peculiar that I couldn't stop myself from asking, 'Allen, what's wrong?'

"Your father just walked away from me. That's what he did. He turned his back to me and made his way through the people packed around us. 'I'll wait for you,' he called to me over his shoulder, but he didn't say where, and he didn't check to be sure that I'd heard him.

"I thought of following him — at the time, it seemed the correct bride-to-be way of dealing with the situation. I could see his back moving through the crowd; I could even imagine calling after him, *Allen, wait for me!* But as I was about to take my first step in his wake, it came to me that he must be afraid of heights and couldn't bring himself to tell me. I found myself smiling; I knew I had to be right. I got this little rush of affection for him. It didn't make me follow him, but it did let me cast away the last doubt I had about marrying him. Just as that shred of doubt fell away, I realized what a burden it had been.

"In the crowd of people, I stood by myself, feeling as I could never have imagined I'd feel. Underneath my coat, one layer down, I was a girl straight out of the burlesque — and the cold air on my skin kept reminding me of that. I felt naughty, I felt hellacious, I felt scandalous enough to sidle up to some richly dressed gentleman and strike up a conversation. Yet I felt prim and old-fashioned, too, because I'd absolutely settled in my mind that I was going to be Allen Crandall's wife.

"When I started to look for him — this was a comical thing to happen so immediately after my grand conclusion — I couldn't find him. I expected him to be standing near the bank of elevators. I mean, that would be the logical place for a person to wait, wouldn't you think? A couple of times I imagined that I saw his back or his shoulders, but when I'd move to look at the person's face, it wouldn't be Allen's. Even though I knew I was being silly, I nearly panicked. By making myself think hard, I realized that the only thing that would make him feel better was to get completely away from the place that had made him afraid. He must have taken the elevator down. When it became clear in my mind that that's what he'd done, I moved into the elevator with the other people who'd had enough of viewing the city at night.

"Going down without your father beside me, I felt almost ashamed for being nearly naked among those tourists. I'm sure I was blushing when I stepped into the lobby. He was right there where I could see him — leaning against the wall, reading a pamphlet, apparently absorbed in it. But I was so tuned in to him at that instant that I could tell he was only pretending to read and that he'd placed himself there so that I couldn't miss him when I stepped out of the elevator.

"As I moved toward him, I knew I couldn't tell him what I'd realized: that it would be okay for me to marry him. I had this urge to explain that all my doubts had fallen away. And I wanted to tell him that it was because I'd seen him afraid and too proud to tell me what was wrong. But I knew I'd hurt his feelings. So I walked up and gave him a hug that he was too self-conscious to accept gracefully. 'I'm ready to go back now,' I whispered into his stiff arms. I almost started crying when I said it, but even there — because I knew he'd be embarrassed — I held back for your father's sake."

Abruptly, my mother stops speaking, as if she has to think for a moment about what she's just said. Only occasionally has she looked at me all the time she was telling me the story of the dress, but now she's looking straight at me — or maybe straight *through* me. After a moment, she says, very quietly, "I held back for his sake."

I don't want to speak, in case she has more to tell me, but I nod — and that must be what she wants from me, because she sighs and relaxes into her chair, staring at the dress in her lap and moving her fingers over it. I keep still, too. I'm pretty sure I understand what she's telling me about herself and my dad with this story. I also know that this is not the time for us to talk directly about what's happened to the two of them.

"I feel sorry for him; I really do." My mother's voice shakes with emotion now. Looking directly at me again, she says, "But you know what, Suellen? Tonight, right now, sitting here with you, I can't concern myself with that young man and his problems. I have to let him go, because I have this perfectly clear picture of *who I was* that night. I'm leaning a little over the edge of the parapet and facing into the wind. It's just a breeze, just barely enough to push my hair back, but it makes me feel strong — it makes me feel I could lift off and fly over the city."

My mother wants to be left alone. She's been quiet for a while, and she still has the dress in her lap, but I think she's forgotten it's there. Her hands are still; her eyes look straight ahead. I stand up and give her a kiss on the forehead. "Good night, darling," she tells me. She lifts a hand to touch my shoulder, but I know that I'm barely in her thoughts. "Please turn out the hall light as you go up. I'd like to sit here a while."

I do as I'm told, of course, but I'm worried about her. When my dad still lived here, she never sat alone, by herself like this. I don't think it's missing him that bothers her as much as it is the stillness of this house, after its being so lively around here for all those years. Anyone would have a hard time making such an adjustment, even my mother, who, as far as I know, has never been defeated by anything in her whole life.

So I do turn out the hall light and walk up the stairs and go to my room and put on my pajamas. I turn the covers back, sit down on the bed, and turn off the bedside light, before I admit to myself that sleep is out of the question. I keep seeing these pictures of my mother and my father, as young as I am, in New York City. It's truly unsettling. And I know I can't go back downstairs and try to talk to her again, try to get her to tell me more. I get out of bed and walk onto the little balcony outside my sister's room and mine on this side of the house. It's a hot, humid night; the whole neighborhood is humming with air conditioners.

I can't see any stars, but the underwater lights of our pool cast up a soft emerald glow into the darkness. It calms me to watch the ripples across the water's surface. Just as I'm thinking maybe I can get to sleep after all, there comes, from one floor down, a soft, vibrating rumble — the sound of the glass door sliding open.

Directly beneath where I'm standing, my mother walks out onto the patio. It's so peculiar to be looking down on her head and shoulders that I'm tempted to call out to her. I wouldn't even have to raise my voice, she's that near. Her steps are slow, and her head is down. She stops in the middle of the patio and lifts her head as if she wants to see the stars, too. I wonder whether she'll notice me, but she doesn't. She turns toward the neighbors' houses on either side of us, checking them out, I guess. Then she surprises me by having herself a good back-bending, shoulder-popping stretch. That's a positive sign, as far as I'm concerned. I can't see her face, but I know that if she's stretching like that, she's got to be at least half smiling. I know my mother pretty well.

Yet she shocks me with what she does next; in a million years I'd never figure her to pull off that old sweatshirt she's been wearing lately, unzip and step out of her khaki slacks, slip off her bra, and step out of her underpants. As each item comes off, she drops it straight onto the concrete beside her. Then my mother — the midnight stripper! — steps over to the deep end of the pool and stands with her arms at her sides and her toes over the edge. She gazes down into the water.

She just stands there — and it really does make some heat come to my face to see her like this, naked in front of the whole world. I remind myself that the neighbors are asleep and that I'm probably the only one who'd be freaked out by what she's doing. She looks so small down there, so skinny and pale, with that green light shimmering over the front of her body. I don't like thinking that my mother is as vulnerable as she looks right now. I can't remember seeing her without at least a towel wrapped around her. If I ever tell my sister what I'm seeing at this moment, she'll say, "Modest Marcy? I don't think so." Erin just flat out wouldn't believe me. And I wouldn't dream of telling my dad. He'd spend about two hours explaining to me how it wasn't possible for the woman who was his wife to behave this way.

She holds still for so long that she begins to look comfortable, standing there at the edge. It occurs to me that maybe she's enjoying the warm air on her skin. This, too, is strange for me, understanding how my mother could enjoy such a solitary pleasure. How could I ever have thought that I knew all there was to know about that woman down there? All of a sudden, she's a statue come to life. She raises her arms, bends her knees, tilts forward, pushes off, and knifes downward. Under the water, she's a shadow, gliding with her hands arrowed out ahead of her. And when she breaks the surface, she's already moving into her strokes.

© MARION ETTLINGER

David Huddle's fiction, essays, and poetry have appeared in *Esquire, Harper's Magazine, Playboy, Story,* the *New York Times Magazine,* and *The Best American Short Stories.* Among his books of short fiction are *Tenorman, Intimates,* and *Only the Little Bone.* The recipient of two NEA fellowships, he teaches writing at the University of Vermont and is on the faculty of the Bread Loaf School of English.